PENGUIN BOOKS

EMBERS

Sándor Márai was born in Kassa, in the Austro-Hungarian Empire, in 1900 and died in San Diego in 1989. He rose to fame as one of the leading literary novelists in Hungary in the 1930s. Profoundly antifascist, he survived the Second World War, but persecution by the Communists drove him from the country in 1948, first to Italy, then to the United States. He is the author of a body of work now being rediscovered and translated into English.

Carol Brown Janeway's translations include Binjamin Wilkomirski's *Fragments*, Marie de Hennezel's *Intimate Death*, Bernhard Schlink's *The Reader*, Jan Philipp Reemtsma's *In the Cellar*, Hans-Ulrich Treichel's *Lost*, Zvi Kolitz's *Yosl Rakover Talks to God*, Benjamin Lebert's *Crazy* and Yasmina Reza's *Desolation*.

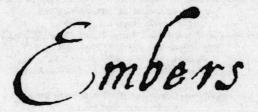

Embers

SÁNDOR MÁRAI

Translated by
Carol Brown Janeway

PENGUIN BOOKS

PENGUIN BOOKS

Published by the Penguin Group
Penguin Books Ltd, 80 Strand, London WC2R ORL, England
Penguin Putnam Inc., 375 Hudson Street, New York, New York 10014, USA
Penguin Books Australia Ltd, 250 Camberwell Road,
Camberwell, Victoria 3124, Australia
Penguin Books Canada Ltd, 10 Alcorn Avenue, Toronto, Ontario, Canada M4V 3B2
Penguin Books India (P) Ltd, 11 Community Centre,
Panchsheel Park, New Delhi – 110 017, India
Penguin Books (NZ) Ltd, Cnr Rosedale and Airborne Roads,
Albany, Auckland, New Zealand
Penguin Books (South Africa) (Pty) Ltd, 24 Sturdee Avenue,
Rosebank 2196, South Africa

Penguin Books Ltd, Registered Offices: 80 Strand, London WC2R ORL, England

www.penguin.com

Originally published in Hungary as *A gyertyák csonkig egnék* 1942
Reprinted by Helikon Kiado, Budapest, 1990
This edition published in Germany as *Die Glut* by Piper Verlag GmbH 1999
This translation of *Die Glut* first published in the
United States of America by Alfred A. Knopf 2001
Published in Great Britain by Viking 2002
Published in Penguin Books 2003

9

Set in Adobe Garamond
Typeset by Rowland Phototypesetting Ltd, Bury St Edmunds, Suffolk
Printed in England by Clays Ltd, St Ives plc

Embers

1

In the morning, the old general spent a considerable time in the wine cellars with his winegrower inspecting two casks of wine that had begun to ferment. He had gone there at first light, and it was past eleven o'clock before he had finished drawing off the wine and returned home. Between the columns of the veranda, which exuded a musty smell from its damp flagstones, his gamekeeper was standing waiting for him, holding a letter.

"What do you want?" the General demanded brusquely, pushing back his broad-brimmed straw hat to reveal a flushed face. For years now, he had neither opened nor read a single letter. The mail went to the estate manager's office, to be sorted and dealt with by one of the stewards.

"It was brought by a messenger," said the gamekeeper, standing stiffly at attention.

The General recognized the handwriting. Taking the letter and putting it in his pocket, he stepped into the cool of the entrance hall and, without uttering a word, handed the gamekeeper both his stick and his hat. He removed a pair of spectacles from his cigar case, went over to the window where light insinuated itself through the slats of the blinds, and began to read.

"Wait," he said over his shoulder to the gamekeeper, who was about to leave the room to dispose of cane and hat.

He crumpled the letter into his pocket. "Tell Kalman to harness up at six o'clock. The Landau, because there's rain in the air. And he is to wear full-dress livery. You too," he said with unexpected force, as if suddenly angered. "Everything must shine. The carriage and harness are to be cleaned immediately. Then put on your livery, and seat yourself next to Kalman on the coachbox. Understood?"

8

"Yes, Excellence," said the gamekeeper, looking his master directly in the eye. "At six o'clock." "At half past six you will leave," said the General, and then appeared to be making some calculation, for his lips moved silently. "You will go to the White Eagle. All you are to say is that I have sent you, and the carriage for the Captain is waiting. Repeat."

The gamekeeper repeated the words. Then the General raised his hand, as if he had just thought of something else, and he looked up at the ceiling but didn't say anything and went upstairs to the second floor. The gamekeeper, still frozen to attention, watched him, unblinking, and waited until the thickset, broad-shouldered figure disappeared around the turn of the stone balustrade.

The General went into his room, washed his hands, and stepped over to his high, narrow standing desk; arranged on its surface of unstained green felt were pens, ink, and a perfectly aligned stack of those notebooks covered in black-and-white-checked oil-cloth commonly used by schoolchildren for their homework. In the middle of the desk stood a green-shaded lamp, which the General switched on, as the room was dark. On the other side of the closed blinds, in the scorched, withered garden, summer ignited a last blaze like an arsonist setting the fields on fire in senseless fury before making his escape. The General took out the letter, carefully smoothed the paper, set his glasses on his nose and placed the sheet under the bright light to read the straight short lines of angular handwriting, his arms folded behind his back.

There was a calendar hanging on the wall. Its fist-sized numbers showed August 14. The General looked up at the ceiling and counted: August 14. July 2. He was calculating how much time had elapsed between that long-ago day and today. "Forty-one years," he said finally, half aloud. Recently he had been talking to himself even when he was alone in the room. "*Forty* years," he then said, confused, and blushed like a schoolboy who's stumbled in the middle of a lesson, tilted his head back and closed his watering eyes. His neck reddened and bulged over the maize-yellow collar of his jacket. "July 2, 1899, was the day of the hunt," he murmured, then fell silent. Propping his elbows on the desk like a student at his studies, he went back to staring anxiously at the letter with its brief handwritten message. "Forty-one," he said again, hoarsely. "And forty-three days. Yes, exactly."

He seemed calmer now, and began to walk up and down. The room had a vaulted ceiling, supported by a central column. It had once been two rooms, a bedroom, and a dressing room.

Many years ago—he thought only in decades, anything more exact upset him, as if he might be reminded of things he would rather forget—he had had the wall between the two rooms torn down. Only the column holding up the central vault remained. The castle had been built two hundred years earlier by an army supplier who sold oats to the Austrian cavalry and in course of time was promoted to the nobility. The General had been born here in this room.

In those days the room farthest back, the dark one that looked onto the garden and estate offices, had been his mother's bedroom, while the lighter, airier room had been the dressing room.

For decades now, since he had moved into this wing of the building, and torn down the dividing wall, this large, shadowy chamber had replaced the two rooms. Seventeen paces from the door to the bed. Eighteen paces from the wall on the garden side to the balcony. Both distances counted off exactly.

He lived here as an invalid lives within the space he has learned to inhabit. As if the room had been tailored to his body. Years passed without him setting foot in the other wing of the castle, in which salon after salon opened one into the next, first green, then blue, then red, all hung with gold chandeliers.

The windows in the south wing gave onto the park with its chestnut trees that stood in a semicircle in front of protruding balustrades held up by fat stone angels, and bowed down over the balconies in spring in all their dark-green magnificence, lit with pink flowering candles. When he went out, it was to the cellars or into the forest or—every morning, rain or shine, even in winter—to the trout pond. And when he came back, he went through the entrance hall and up to his bedroom, and it was here that he ate all his meals.

"So he's come back," he said aloud, standing in the middle of the room. "Forty-one years and forty-three days later."

These words seemed suddenly to exhaust him, as

if he had only just understood the enormousness of forty-one years and forty-three days. He swayed, then sat down in the leather armchair with its worn back. On the little table within reach of his hand was a little silver bell, which he rang.

"Tell Nini to come up here," he said to the servant. And then, politely, "If she'd be so kind."

2

*N*ini was ninety-one years old. She came at once. She had rocked the General in his cradle in this room. She had stood in this room as the General was being born. She had been sixteen then, and very beautiful. Small, but so well-muscled and calm that her body seemed possessed of a secret, as if her bones, her flesh, her blood concealed within them some essence, the secret of time or of life itself, a secret that could neither be told nor translated into any language, since it was beyond words. She was the daughter of the village postmaster, she was sixteen when she gave birth to a child, and no one ever discovered the identity of the father. When her father beat her and threw her out of the house, she came to the castle and suckled the newborn child, because her milk was plentiful. She came with no possessions other than the dress on her back and a lock of hair, tucked in an envelope, from her dead baby. That was how she presented herself at the castle. She came in time for the birth. The General had his first taste of milk at Nini's breast.

So she lived in the castle silently for seventy-five years. Silent and smiling. Her name flew through the rooms as if the inhabitants of the castle were trying to draw one another's attention to something. "Nini," they said, as if to say, "How extraordinary that there's more in the world than egoism, passion, vanity. Nini . . ." And because she was always in the right place, nobody ever saw her; and because she was always good-humored, nobody ever asked her how it was that she could always be good-humored when the man she loved had abandoned her and the child who should have drunk her milk was dead. She suckled the General and raised him, and seventy-five years went by. From time to time the sun shone over the castle and the family, and at such moments of universal well-being people were surprised to notice that Nini was smiling too. Then the Countess, the General's mother, died, and Nini took a cloth soaked in vinegar and washed the cold, white, sweat-streaked forehead of the corpse. And then one day they brought the father of the General back home on a stretcher, for he had fallen from his horse. He lived for another five years, and Nini took care of him. She read French books aloud to him, saying each letter because she couldn't speak the language, and stringing them together until the invalid made sense of them. Then the General got married, and when the couple returned from their honeymoon, Nini was standing waiting for them at the entrance. She kissed the hand of the new countess and offered her roses, again with a smile. It was a moment that the General remembered from time to time. Then after twelve years the new countess died, and Nini tended the grave and the clothes of the dead woman.

She had neither rank nor title in the household. Everyone simply recognized her strength. Aside from the General, nobody knew that she was over ninety. It was never a topic of conversation. Nini's was a power that surged through the house, the people in it, the walls, the objects, the way some invisible galvanic current animates Punch and the Policeman on the stage at a little traveling puppet show. Sometimes people had the feeling that the house and its contents could, like ancient fabrics, fall apart at a touch and crumble to nothing if Nini were not there to hold them together with her strength. After his wife died, the General went on a long journey. When he returned a year later, he moved into his mother's room in the old wing of the castle. The new wing, in which he had lived with his wife, the brilliantly colored salons with their French silk wall-coverings already fraying, the great reception room with its fireplace and its books, the staircase with its antlers, stuffed grouse, and mounted chamois heads, the large dining room with its view from the window down the valley and over the little town to the distant silver-blue shapes of the mountains, his wife's room and his own bedroom next door, were all closed and locked at his orders. For thirty-two years following the death of his wife and his return from abroad, the only people to enter these rooms were Nini and the servants when they cleaned them every two months.

"Sit down, Nini," said the General.

The nurse sat down. In the last year she had become old. After reaching ninety, one ages differently from the way one aged at fifty or sixty: one ages without bitterness. Nini's face was rose pink and crumpled—such is the way noble fabrics age, and centuries-old silks that hold woven in their threads the assembled skills and dreams of an entire family. The previous year she had developed a cataract in one eye, leaving it gray and sad. The other eye had remained blue, the timeless blue of a mountain lake in August, and it smiled. Nini was dressed as always in dark blue, dark-blue felt skirt, simple blouse. As if she hadn't had any new clothes made in the last seventy-five years.

"Konrad has written," said the General, holding up the letter. "Do you remember?"

"Yes," said Nini. She remembered it all. "He's here in the town," said the General very quietly, the way one conveys a piece of information that is of utmost importance and extremely confidential. "He's staying at the White Eagle. He's coming here tonight, I'm sending the carriage to bring him. He will dine here."

"Where here?" asked Nini calmly, allowing her blue eye, the living, smiling eye, to cast its gaze around the room.

For the last twenty years, no one had been received here. The visitors who sometimes arrived at lunchtime, gentlemen from the regional government and the city council, or guests who had come for one of the great shoots, were received by the steward in the hunting lodge that was kept ready no matter what the time of year; everything was organized for their welcome: bedchambers, bathrooms, kitchen, the large informal hunters' dining room, the open veranda, the rustic wooden tables. On such occasions the steward presided at the head of the table and extended hospitality to the hunters and officials in the name of the General. Nobody was in any way offended by this, everyone knew that the master of the house did not appear in public. The only person to enter the castle was the priest, who came once a year, in winter, to inscribe in chalk the initials of Caspar, Melchior, and Balthazar on the doorframe. The priest, who had presided at the funerals of the family. Aside from him, no one. Ever.

"The other side," said the General. "Can that be done?"

"We cleaned it a month ago," said the nurse, "so it surely can be done."

"Eight o'clock. Can it be done? . . ." he asked again anxiously, in an almost childlike way, leaning forward in his chair. "In the great dining hall. It's noon already."

"Noon," said the nurse. "I will give the instructions. Air the rooms until six o'clock, then set the table." She moved her lips silently, as if counting up the time and the tasks to be completed, then said yes with quick confidence.

Still leaning forward, the General watched her closely. Their two lives were slowly trundling and bumping along their way, inextricably linked in the rhythms of great old age. Each knew everything about the other, more than mother and child, more than husband and wife. The intimacy that bound them was closer than any physical bond. Perhaps it was a matter of mother's milk. Perhaps because Nini had been the first person to see the General as he was born, at the moment of his delivery, in the blood and slime that accompany all mankind into the world. Perhaps because of the seventy-five years they had lived under the same roof, eating the same food, breathing the same air, sharing the slightly musty atmosphere of the house and the same view of the trees outside the windows. And all of it lay too deep for words. They were neither brother and sister nor lovers. But there are other ties, numinous ones, and of these they were aware. There is a kind of consanguinity both closer and more powerful than that of twins in a mother's womb. Life had melded their days and their nights, each knew the other's body just as each knew the other's dreams. The nurse said, "Do you want it to be the way it used to be?"

"Yes," said the General. "Exactly the same. The way it was last time."

"Very well," was all she said.

She went to him, bent down to his old man's hand with its age spots, its knotted veins and its signet ring, and kissed it.

"Promise me you won't get upset," she said. "I promise," was the General's soft and docile reply.

3

Until five o'clock there was no sign of life from the room. Then he rang for his servant and ordered a cold bath. He had sent back his midday meal and drunk no more than a lukewarm cup of tea. He lay in the dim light of the room on a divan. Beyond the cool walls, summer buzzed and hummed and seethed. Like a spy he took note of the boiling restlessness of the light, the rustle of the hot wind in the desiccated leaves, and the noises of the castle.

Now that the first surprise had passed, he suddenly felt tired. One spends a lifetime preparing for something. First one suffers the wound. Then one plans revenge. And waits. He had been waiting a long time now. He no longer knew when it was that the wound had become a thirst for revenge, and the thirsting had turned to waiting. Time preserves everything, but as it does so, it fades things to the colorlessness of ancient photographs fixed on metal plates. Light and time erase the contours and distinctive shading of the faces. One has to angle the image this way and that until it catches the light in a particular way and one can make out the person whose features have been absorbed into the blank surface of the plate. It is the same with our memories. But then one day light strikes from a certain angle and one recaptures a face again. The General had a drawer of old photographs like that. The one of his father. Dressed in the uniform of a captain of the guards, with his hair in thick curls, like a girl. Around his shoulders, a white guard's cape, which he held together against his chest with one hand, rings flashing. His head tilted to one side with an air of offended pride. He had never spoken of where and how he had been offended. When he returned from Vienna, he went hunting. Day after day, hunt after hunt, no matter what the time of year; if it was neither the season for red deer nor other game, he hunted foxes and crows.

As if he were set on killing someone and was keeping himself ready at any moment to take his revenge. The Countess, the General's mother, would not have the huntsmen in the castle, she banned and banished anything and everything associated with hunting—weapons, cartridge pouches, old arrows, stuffed birds and stags' heads, antlers. That was when the Captain of the Guards had the hunting lodge built. It became the place for everything: great bearskins in front of the fireplace, panels framed in brown wood and draped in white felt on the walls to display weapons. Belgian and Austrian guns. English knives, Russian bullet holders. Something for every type of game. The kennels were nearby, the entire pack and the tracking dogs and the Vizslas and the falconer lived there with his three hooded falcons. Here in the hunting lodge was where the General's father spent his time. The inhabitants of the castle saw him only at mealtimes. The castle interiors were all in pastels, the walls hung with coverings of pale blue, pale green, and soft rose striped with gold, from workshops near Paris. Every year the Countess herself would select papers and furniture from French manufacturers and shops, when she went to visit her family. She never failed to make this journey, which was guaranteed to her in her marriage contract when she accepted the hand of the foreign Officer of the Guards.

"Perhaps it was all because of those journeys," thought the General.

He thought this because his parents had not had an easy marriage. The Officer of the Guards went hunting, and because he could not destroy the world of other places and other people—foreign cities, Paris, castles, foreign tongues, foreign manners—he slaughtered bears, deer, and stags. Yes, perhaps it was because of the journeys. He got to his feet and stood in front of the sway-bellied white porcelain stove that once had warmed his mother's bedroom. It was a large stove, at least a century old, and it radiated heat like some indolent corpulent gentleman intent on mitigating his own egoism with an easy act of charity. Clearly his mother had always suffered from the cold here. This castle in the depths of the forest with its vaulted rooms was too dark for her; hence the light-colored silks on the walls. And she froze, because there was always a wind in the forest, even in summer, bringing with it the smell of mountain streams when they fill with the melting snow and run in spates, flooding their banks. She froze, and the white stove was kept burning all the time. She was waiting for a miracle. She had come to Eastern Europe because the passion she felt had overwhelmed her reason. The Officer of the Guards had made her acquaintance on a tour of duty when he was diplomatic courier at the embassy in Paris in the 1850s. They were introduced to each other at a ball, and somehow this meeting had an aura of inevitability. The music played and the Officer of the Guards said in French to the Count's daughter, "In our country feelings are more intense and more decisive." It was the embassy ball. Outside, the street was white; it was snowing. At this moment the Emperor of France made his entrance into the ballroom. Everyone made a deep obeisance. The Emperor's dress coat was blue and his waistcoat white; slowly he raised his gold lorgnon to his eyes. As they both straightened up again, their eyes met. Already they knew that their lives must be together. Pale and self-conscious, they smiled at each other.

Music could be heard from the next room. The young French girl said, "Your country—where is it?" and smiled again with a faraway look. The Officer of the Guards told her the name of his homeland. It was the first intimate word to pass between them.

It was autumn when they came home, almost a year later. The foreign lady sat deep inside the coach, swathed in veils and coverlets. They took the mountain route across Switzerland and the Tyrol. In Vienna they were received by the Emperor and Empress. The Emperor was benevolent, just the way he was always described in children's textbooks. "Beware," he said. "In the forest where he's taking you, there are bears. He's a bear too." And he smiled. Everyone smiled. It was a sign of great favor that the Emperor should joke with the French wife of the Hungarian Officer of the Guards. "Majesty," she replied, "I shall tame him with music, as Orpheus tamed the wild beast." They journeyed on through fruit-scented meadows and woods. After they crossed the frontier, mountains and cities dwindled away, and the lady began to weep. "Darling, I feel dizzy. There is no end to all of this." It was the Puszta that made her dizzy, the deserted plain stretching away under the numbing, shimmering blanket of autumn air, now bare after the harvest, transected by primitive roads along which they jolted for hour after hour, while cranes wheeled in the empty sky and the fields of maize on either side lay plundered and broken as if a retreating army had passed through at the end of a war, leaving the landscape a wasteland. The Officer of the Guards sat silently in the coach, his arms crossed. From time to time he ordered a horse to be brought, and he rode for long distances alongside the carriage, observing his native land as if he were seeing it for the first time. He looked at the low houses, with their green shutters and white verandas, where they spent the nights, Magyar houses with their thick-planted gardens all around them, the cool rooms in which every piece of furniture, even the smell in the cupboards, was familiar to him, and the landscape whose melancholy solitude moved him as never before. He saw with his wife's eyes the wells with their hanging buckets, the parched fields, the rosy clouds above the plain in the sunset. His homeland opened itself before them, and with a beating heart the officer sensed that the landscape that now embraced them also held the secret of their fate. His wife sat in the coach and said nothing. Sometimes she raised a handkerchief to her face, and as she did so, her husband would bend down toward her out of the saddle and cast a questioning glance into her tear-filled eyes. But with a gesture she signaled that they should continue. Their lives were joined together now.

At first the castle was a comfort to her. It was so large, and the forest and the mountains wrapped themselves around it to isolate it so completely from the plain that it seemed to her to be a home within a new and foreign homeland. And every month a wagon from Paris, from Vienna, would arrive bringing furniture, linens, damasks, engravings, even a spinet, because she wished to tame the wild beasts with music. The first snow was already on the mountains as they finally settled in and began to live their lives there; it surrounded the castle and laid siege to it like a grim northern army. At night deer and stags slipped out of the forest to stand motionless under the moonlight in the snow, heads cocked as they observed the lighted windows with their grave animal eyes that gave back a mysterious blue glow, and the music escaping from the castle reached their ears. "Do you see them?" said the young woman as she sat at the keyboard, and laughed. In February the cold drove the wolves down out of the mountains; the servants and the huntsmen built a bonfire of brushwood in the park, and the wolves, under its spell, circled it and howled. The Officer of the Guards drew a knife and went after them; his wife watched from the window. There was something insurmountable between them. But they loved each other.

The General moved to stand before the portrait of his mother. It was the work of a Viennese artist who had also painted the Empress with her hair down, gathered into loose plaits. The Officer of the Guards had seen this portrait in the Emperor's study in the Hofburg. In the portrait the Countess was wearing a rose-colored straw hat decorated with flowers, the kind of hat the girls of Florence wear in the summer. The painting in its gold frame hung over the cherry-wood chest with its many drawers, which had also belonged to his mother. The General set both hands on it as he leaned to look up at the work of the Viennese artist. The young woman held her head to one side, gazing gravely and softly into the distance as if posing a question that was in itself the message of the picture. Her features were noble, her neck, her hands in their crocheted gloves and her forearms as sensual as her white shoulders and the sweep of her décolleté. She did not belong here. The battle between husband and wife was fought without words. Their weapons were music, hunting, travels, and evening receptions, when the castle was lit up as if it were on fire, the stables were jammed with horses and carriages, and on every fourth step of the great staircase a *heiduch* stood as stiff as a mannequin holding up a twelve-armed silver candelabrum, while melodies, light, voices and the scent of bodies swirled through the rooms as if life itself were a desperate feast, a sublime and tragic celebration that would end when the horns rang out to announce an unholy summons to the assembled guests. The General could remember evenings like that. Sometimes the coachmen and their horses had to make camp around the bonfires in the snowy park because the stables were full. And once even the Emperor came, although in this country he bore the title of King. He came in a carriage, escorted by horsemen with white plumes in their helmets. He stayed for two days, went hunting in the forest, lived in the other wing of the castle, slept in an iron bedstead, and danced with the lady of the house. As they danced, they talked together and the young wife's eyes filled with tears. The King stopped dancing, bowed, kissed her hand, and led her into the next room, where his entourage was standing in a semicircle. He led her to the Officer of the Guards and kissed her hand again.

"What did you talk about?" the Officer of the Guards asked his wife later, much later.

But his wife did not say. Nobody ever learned what the King had said to the young wife who had come from a foreign country and wept as she danced. It went on being a local topic of conversation for a long time.

*T*he castle was a closed world, like a great granite mausoleum full of the moldering bones of generations of men and women from earlier times, in their shrouds of slowly disintegrating gray silk or black cloth. It enclosed silence itself as if it were a prisoner persecuted for his beliefs, wasting away numbly, unshaven and in rags on a pile of musty rotting straw in a dungeon. It also enclosed memories as if they were the dead, memories that lurked in damp corners the way mushrooms, bats, rats, and beetles lurk in the mildewed cellars of old houses. Door-latches gave off the traces of a once-trembling hand, the excitement of a moment long gone, so that even now another hand hesitated to press down on them. Every house in which passion has loosed itself on people in all its fury exudes such intangible presences.

The General looked at the portrait of his mother. He knew every feature of the narrow, fine-boned face. The eyes gazed down through time with sad and somnolent disdain. It was the look with which women of an earlier era had mounted the scaffold, scorning both those for whom they were giving their lives and those who were taking their lives from them. His mother's family owned a castle in Brittany, by the sea. The General must have been about eight years old the summer he was taken there. By this time they were able to travel by train, albeit very slowly. The suitcases in their linen covers embroidered with his mother's initials swayed in the luggage nets. In Paris, it was raining. The child sat in a carriage upholstered in blue silk, looking through the hazy glass of the windows at the city glistening in the raindrops like the slippery underbelly of a great fish. He saw the rearing outlines of roofs and great chimneys that slanted up against the dirty curtains of wet sky, seeming to prophesy the secret truths of unfamiliar and unknowable fates. Women walked laughing through the downpour, lifting their skirts with one hand, their teeth glinting as if the rain, the strange city, and the French language were something both wonderful and comic that only the child failed to comprehend. He was eight years old and sat gravely in the coach beside his mother, facing the maid and the governess, sensing that some task had been imposed upon him. Everyone's eyes were on him, the little savage from a faraway country, from the forest with the bears. He articulated his French words with circumspect deliberation and care. He was aware that now he spoke for his father, the castle, the hounds, the forest, and the entire homeland he had left behind. A great gate opened, the carriage entered a large courtyard, French servants made their bows in front of a broad staircase. It all felt a little hostile. He was led through rooms in which everything occupied its own painfully meticulous and intimidating space. In the large salon on the second floor he was received by his French grandmother. Her eyes were gray and there was a black shadow on her upper lip; her hair, which must once have been red but now was a dirty non-color, as if time itself had forgotten to wash it, was piled high on her head. She kissed the child and with her bony white hands tilted his head back a little so that she could gaze down into his face. "Tout de même," she said to his mother, who was standing beside him anxiously, as if he were taking an examination that was about to reveal something.

Later, lime-blossom tisane was brought. Everything smelled so strange that the child felt faint. Round about midnight he began to weep and vomit. "I want Nini," he cried, his voice choked with sobs as he lay in bed, deathly pale.

Next day, he was running a high fever and was incoherent. Solemn doctors arrived wearing black frock coats with watch chains fixed into the middle buttonhole of their white waistcoats; as they bent over the child, their beards and clothes exuded the same smell as the furnishings of the palace, which was also the smell of his grandmother's hair and the smell on her breath. He thought he would die if the smell didn't go away. By the end of the week his fever still had not abated and his pulse was weakening. That was when they telegraphed for Nini.

It took four days for the nurse to reach Paris.

The muttonchop-whiskered majordomo failed to recognize her at the station, and so she set off on foot to the palace, carrying her traveling bag made of crochet work. She arrived like a migrating bird. She spoke no French, she did not know the streets, and she was never able to explain how in the middle of the strange city she had found the palace and her sick charge. She came into the room and lifted the dying child out of his bed; his body was no longer moving, only his eyes glittered. She set him in her lap, held him tight in her arms and gently began to rock him. On the third day he was given extreme unction. That evening, Nini came out of the sick-room and said in Hungarian to the Countess, "I think he is going to pull through."

She shed no tears, she was merely exhausted after six nights without sleep. She took some food from home out of the crocheted bag and began to eat. For six days she kept the child alive by the power of her breath. The Countess kneeled outside the door, weeping and praying. Everyone was with her—the

French grandmother, the servants, a young priest with slanted eyebrows who came and went at all hours.

The doctors' visits tapered off. The mother and son left for Brittany, taking Nini, but leaving the grandmother behind in Paris, shocked and hurt. Of course, nobody uttered a word about the cause of the child's illness, but everybody knew: the boy needed love, and when all the strangers had bent over him and the unbearable smell had surrounded him on all sides, he had chosen death. In Brittany the wind sang and the waves churned against the age-old rocks. Red cliffs rose up out of the sea. Nini, calm and assured, smiled at the ocean and the sky as if they were already familiar to her. The four corners of the castle were surmounted by ancient turrets of undressed stone from which the Countess's ancestors had kept watch against Surcouf the pirate. The boy was soon brown from the sun and full of laughter. He was no longer afraid: he knew that the two of them, he and Nini, were the strong ones. They sat on the sand, the frills on Nini's dress blew in the wind, and everything smelled of salt, not just the air but the flowers, too. When the tide went out in the mornings, they found sea spiders with hairy legs in the crevices of the red rocks, and crabs with red stomachs and star-shaped jelly fish.

In the castle courtyard there was an incredibly ancient fig tree that looked like some oriental sage who only had the simplest of stories left to tell. Its leaves made a thick canopy for the cool, sweet air underneath.

In the middle of the day, when the sea was no more than a muffled grumble, the nurse would sit here quietly with the child.

"I want to be a poet," the boy said once, glancing up obliquely.

He stared at the sea, his blond curls stirring in the warm wind and his eyes, half-closed, interrogating the horizon. The nurse put her arms around him and squeezed his head against her breast. "No, you're going to be a soldier."

"Like Father?" The child shook his head. "Father is a poet too, didn't you know? He's always thinking about something else."

"That's true," said the nurse with a sigh. "Don't go into the sun, my angel, it'll give you a headache."

They sat for a long time under the fig tree,

listening to the familiar roaring of the sea. It was the same sound made by the forest back home. The child and the nurse thought about the world and how everything in it is related.

5

*I*t is the kind of idea that comes later to most people. Decades pass, one walks through a darkened room in which someone has died, and suddenly one recalls long forgotten words and the roar of the sea. It's as if those few words had captured the whole meaning of life, but afterwards one always talks about something else.

When they made the journey home from Brittany in the fall, the Officer of the Guards was waiting for them in Vienna. The child was enrolled in the military academy. He received a little sword, long trousers, and a shako. The sword was buckled onto him, and on Sundays he and the other cadets were taken for walks along the Graben in their dark-blue tunics. They looked like children playing soldiers. They wore white gloves and gave charming salutes.

The military academy was situated on a hill just outside Vienna. It was a yellow-painted building, and from the windows on the third floor one could see the old city with its streets running straight as a die, and the Emperor's summer palace, the roofs of Schönbrunn, and the paths bordered by pleached trees. In the white corridors with their vaulted ceilings, in the classrooms, the dining hall, and the dormitories, everything was so reassuringly *there* that this seemed to be the only place on earth where every object that otherwise was disorderly or superfluous in life finally was brought into harmony and proper function. The instructors were old officers. Everything smelled of saltpeter. Every dormitory housed thirty children of roughly the same age who slept on narrow iron beds, just like the Emperor. Over the door hung a crucifix decorated with a twig of willow blessed with holy water. A blue night-light burned in the darkness. In the mornings, they were wakened by a bugle call. In winter, the water in the tin washbasins was sometimes frozen over; when that happened, the adjutants fetched cans of warm water from the kitchen.

They learned Greek, and ballistics, and the proper comportment of a soldier in battle, and history. The child was pale, and coughed. In fall the chaplain took him for a walk each afternoon in Schönbrunn, strolling down the allée. Where a fountain gushed out of crumbling moss-covered moldered stones, the water made a stream of gold in the sun. They walked between the rows of pleached trees, the boy conscious of his bearing, raising his white gloved hand in a stiff, correct salute to the veterans who came by in their dress uniforms as if every day were the Emperor's birthday. Once, a woman came from the opposite direction, head bare, a white lace parasol on her shoulder; she was walking rapidly, and as she passed them the chaplain bowed deeply.

"The Empress," he whispered to the child. The woman was very pale and she wore her heavy black hair in a plait that was wound three times round her head. She was followed, three steps behind, by a lady dressed in black and a little hunched, as if she were exhausted by the pace that had been set.

"The Empress," the chaplain said again, reverently. The child looked after the tall lady who was almost running down the allée of the great park as if she were fleeing something.

"She looks like Mama," said the child, thinking of the portrait that hung in his father's study over the table.

"One may not say such things," replied the chaplain reproachfully.

From morning until night, they learned what may and may not be said. The academy with its four hundred pupils was like an infernal machine whose silence presages the explosion to come. They had all been gathered here, the sandy-haired snub-nosed boys with limp white hands from Czech palaces, boys from Moravian estates, boys from fortresses in the Tyrol and hunting lodges in Steiermark, from shuttered palaces in Vienna and country seats in Hungary. All of them bore long names with many consonants and Christian names, titles, and indicators of rank, which had to be given up and handed over in the cloakroom of the academy along with the beautifully tailored civilian clothes made in Vienna and London and the fine underwear from Holland. All that was left was a name and the child belonging to that name, who now must learn what may and may not be said. There were young Slavs with narrow foreheads, whose blood mingled all the human particularities of the Empire, there were blue-eyed weary ten-year-old aristocrats who stared into the distance as if their ancestors had already done all their seeing for them, and there was a Tyrolean duke who shot himself at the age of twelve because he was in love with his cousin.

Konrad slept in the next bed. They were ten years old when they met.

He was squarely built and yet thin, in the manner of those ancient races in which the building of bone mass has taken precedence over the flesh. He was slow moving but not lazy, and he had a rhythm —self-aware yet reserved—all his own. His father, an official in Galicia, had been made a baron; his mother was Polish. When he laughed, his mouth became wide and childlike, giving a slightly Slav cast to his face. But he laughed seldom. He was silent and watchful.

From the first moment, they lived together like twins in their mother's womb. For this they had no need of one of those pacts of the kind that is common among boys of their age, who swear friendship with comical solemn rituals and the sort of portentous intensity invoked by people when for the first time they experience, in unconscious and distorted form, the need to remove another human being from the world, body and soul, and make him uniquely theirs. For that is the hidden force within both friendship and love. Their friendship was deep and wordless, as are all the emotions that will last a lifetime. And like all great emotions, this one contained within itself both shame and a sense of guilt, for no one may isolate one of his fellows from the rest of humanity with impunity.

They knew from the first moment that their meeting would impose upon them lifetime obligations. The young Hungarian boy was tall and slender in those days, and frail, and received weekly visits from the doctor. There was concern about his lungs. At the request of the head of the academy, a colonel from Moravia, the Officer of the Guards came to Vienna for a long conference with the doctors. In all their pronouncements he understood one single word: "Danger." The boy is not really ill, they said, but he has a predisposition to illness. "There's a danger," was the gist of it. The Officer of the Guards had gone to the King of Hungary Hotel in a dark side street in the shadow of St. Stephen's Cathedral; his grandfather had stayed there before him. The corridors were hung with antlers. The hotel manservant bowed and kissed the officer's hand in greeting. The officer took two large, dark, vaulted rooms filled with furniture upholstered in yellow silk, and brought the child to stay with him for the duration of his visit; they lived together in the hotel, where above every door stood the names of favorite regular guests, as if the place were a worldly retreat for lonely servants of the monarchy.

In the mornings they took the carriage and drove out to the Prater. It was the beginning of November and the air was already cool. In the evenings they went to the theater, where heroes gesticulated and declaimed onstage before throwing themselves on their swords and expiring with a death rattle. Afterwards, they ate in a private room in a restaurant, attended by countless waiters. The child sat wordlessly beside his father, conducting himself with precocious good breeding, as if there were something he must bear and forgive.

"They talk about danger," his father said, half to himself, after dinner was over and he was lighting himself a thick black cigar. "If you like, you can come home. But I would prefer it if no danger had the power to make you afraid."

"I'm not afraid, Father," said the child. "But I would like to have Konrad stay with us always. They're poor. I would like him to spend his summers with us."

"Is he your friend?" asked his father.

"Yes."

"Then he is my friend too," said his father seriously.

He was wearing tails and a shirt with a pleated front. In recent times he had set aside his uniform. The boy fell silent, relieved. His father's word was to be trusted. Wherever they went in Vienna, no matter to which shop, he was known: at the tailor's, the glover's, the shirtmaker's, in restaurants where imposing maîtres d'hôtel reigned over the tables and on the street, where gentlemen and ladies waved to him warmly from their carriages.

"Are you going to the Emperor?" the child asked one day shortly before his father was due to depart.

"The King," his father corrected him severely. Then he said, "I don't go to him anymore," and the boy understood that something must have happened between the two of them. On the day his father was leaving, he introduced Konrad to his father. The evening before, he had fallen asleep with a pounding heart: it was like a betrothal. "One may not mention the King in his presence," he warned his friend. But his father was amiable, warm, the perfect gentleman. He welcomed Konrad into the family with one single handshake.

From that day on, the boy coughed less. He was no longer alone. To be alone among people was unbearable to him.

Everything—his life at home, the forest, Paris, his mother's temperament—had fed into his very bloodstream the tendency never to speak of whatever caused him pain but to bear it in silence. He had learned that words are best avoided. But he could not live without love, either, and that was also part of his inheritance. Perhaps it was his French mother who had brought with her the yearning to share her feelings if even with only one other human being. In his father's family, one never spoke of such things. The boy needed someone to love, whether it be Nini or Konrad. His fever went away, as did his cough, and his thin pale child's face flushed with delight and rewarded trust. They were at an age when boys have not yet developed any pronounced sexual identity: it is as if they have not yet chosen. He hated his soft blond hair, because he considered it girlish, and he had the barber cut it short every two weeks. Konrad was more masculine, more composed. Childhood was no longer a cramped place, it no longer intimidated them, because they were no longer alone.

At the end of the first summer, when the boys climbed into the carriage for the journey back to Vienna, the French *maman* stood in the gateway of the castle, looking after them. Then she smiled and said to Nini, "At last—a happy marriage!"

But Nini didn't smile back. Each summer, the boys arrived together. Later they also spent Christmas at the castle. Everything they had was the same: clothes, underwear, they slept in the same room, they

y b

read the same books, together they discovered Vienna and the forest, books and hunting, riding and the military virtues, the life of society and love. Nini worried, and perhaps she was also a little jealous. When the friendship was four years old, the boys began to shut themselves off from other people and to have their own secrets. The relationship steadily deepened, and also became more hermetic. The boy made clear that he wished he could present Konrad to the whole world as his own creation, his masterpiece, yet at other times he watched over him jealously, afraid that someone could rob him of the person he loved.

"It's too much," said Nini to his mother. "One day Konrad will leave him, and he will suffer dreadfully."

"That is our human fate," said his mother. She was sitting at her mirror, staring at her fading beauty. "One day we lose the person we love. Anyone who is unable to sustain that loss fails as a human being and does not deserve our sympathy."

In the academy, the boys' friendship soon ceased to be a subject for mockery; it became accepted as a natural phenomenon. They were given a single name, "the Henriks," like a married couple, but nobody laughed at the relationship; there was some quality—a gentleness, a seriousness, an unconditional generosity—that radiated from it and silenced all tormentors.

All societies recognize these relationships instinctively and envy them; men yearn for disinterested friendship and usually they yearn in vain. The boys in the academy took refuge in family pride or in their studies, in precocious debauchery or physical prowess, in the confusions of premature and painful infatuations. In this emotional turbulence the friendship between Konrad and Henrik had the glow of a quiet and ceremonial oath of loyalty in the Middle Ages.

Nothing is so rare in the young as a disinterested bond that demands neither aid nor sacrifice. Boys always expect a sacrifice from those who are the standard-bearers of their hopes. The two friends felt that they were living in a miraculous and unnamable state of grace.

There is nothing to equal the delicacy of such a relationship. Everything that life has to offer later, sentimental yearnings or raw desire, intense feelings and eventually the bonds of passion, will all be coarser, more barbaric. Konrad was as serious and as discreet at the age of ten as a full-grown man. As the boys grew older and more aware and tried to put on airs and uncover the grown-ups' secrets, Konrad made his friend swear that they would remain chaste. They remained true to this vow for a long time. It was not easy. Every two weeks they went to confession with a list they had compiled together of their sins. Carnal appetites were stirring in blood and nerves, the boys were pale, as the seasons changed they felt dizzy. But they remained chaste, as if their friendship, which lay like a magic cape over their young lives, was a replacement for everything that tormented the others in their curiosity and rest-lessness and drove them toward the darker, lower sides of life.

They lived in a discipline whose roots were deep in centuries-old experience and practice. Every morning they fenced for an hour in the academy gymnasium, bare-chested with masks and bandages. Then they went riding. Henrik was a good horse-man, Konrad struggled desperately to keep his seat and his balance, having no inherited physical skill in the saddle. Henrik learned easily, Konrad with difficulty, but whatever he learned he husbanded with almost desperate zeal; he seemed to know that this would be his only earthly possession. In society, Henrik moved with easy grace and the inner assurance of one whom nothing can surprise; Konrad was awkward and excessively correct. One summer when they were already young men, they traveled to Galicia to visit Konrad's parents. The Baron, a bald, modest old man, worn down by forty years of service in the province and the disappointed social ambitions of his aristocratic Polish wife, endeavored with perplexed eagerness to entertain the young men. The town was depressing with its old towers, its fountain in the center of the rectangular main square, and its dark, vaulted interiors. The inhabitants—Ukrainians, Germans, Jews, Russians—lived in a kind of turmoil that was continually being smothered and contained by the authorities; something seemed to be fermenting in the dimly lit, airless apartments, some uprising or perhaps just an ongoing seditious muttering and wretched discontent, or perhaps not even that, merely the uneasy disorder and permanent restlessness of a caravanserai. It made itself felt in the houses, in the streets, in the entire public life of the town. Only the cathedral with its great tower and its broad arches soared calmly over the hubbub of calls and yells and whispers, as if a single law had once solemnly imposed itself—irreversibly, incontrovertibly, conclusively—on the community. The youths were staying at the inn, for the Baron's apartment contained only three small rooms. The first evening, after the elaborate dinner with its rich meat dishes and heavy aromatic wines, which Konrad's father, the elderly official, and his sad Polish wife —who had painted her face with lilac shadows and powdered blush to overcome her faded looks until she took on the air of a tropical bird—had had served in the humble apartment with touching solicitude, as if the fortunes of their son, who so rarely returned home, depended on the quality of the meal, the young officers returned to their Galician guesthouse and sat for a long time in a dark corner of the dining room with its dust-covered ornamental palms.

"Now you have seen them," said Konrad.

"Yes," said the son of the Officer of the Guards, conscience-stricken.

"So now you know," the other replied, softly and earnestly. "Now you can have some idea of what has been done here for the last twenty-two years for my sake."

"Yes," said the son of the Officer of the Guards, and something in his throat tightened.

"Every pair of gloves," said Konrad, "that I have to buy when we all go to the Burg Theater, comes from here. If I need a new bridle, they do not eat meat for three days. If I leave a tip at an evening party, my father gives up his cigars for a week. That is how it has been for twenty-two years. And I have never lacked for anything. Somewhere, far away in Poland, we had a farmstead. I have never seen it. It belonged to my mother. It was the source of everything: the uniform, school fees, the money for theater tickets, the bouquet I sent to your mother when she passed through Vienna, the entry fees for exams, the costs of the duel I had to fight with that Bavarian. Twenty-two years—all of it. First, they sold the furniture, then the garden, then the surrounding land, then the house. Then, they sacrificed their health, their comfort, their peace, their old age, and my mother's social ambition, which was to have an extra room in this rat-hole of a town, a room with nice furniture where they could receive people from time to time. Do you understand?"

"I ask your pardon," said Henrik, white and shaken.

"I am not angry at you," said his friend with emphatic seriousness. "I only wanted you to see it all once, and understand. When the Bavarian came at me with his drawn sword and started lunging and feinting in all directions like a lunatic, as if he were entertaining himself and as if our attempts to slash and cripple each other out of pure vanity were nothing but a huge joke, I suddenly saw my mother's face, saw her walking to the market every day for fear that the cook might overcharge her by two fillers, because at the end of a year the two fillers all add up to five florins, which she can send me in an envelope . . . and I literally wanted to kill the Bavarian who wanted to injure me out of sheer bravado, and had no idea that anything he might do to me would be a mortal offense against two people in Galicia who have sacrificed their lives for me without a word. When I'm staying with you and I tip one of the servants, I am expending a portion of their lives. It is very hard to live in such a way," he said, and blushed.

"Why?" the other asked softly. "Do you not think that it does them good? Perhaps, for them, perhaps, it does."

The young man fell silent. He had never spoken about any of this before. Now, faltering, without looking up, he said, "It is very hard for me to live in this fashion. It is as if I do not belong to myself. If I fall ill, I am hounded by the feeling that I am squandering someone else's property, something that is not fully mine, namely my health. I am a soldier, I have been trained to kill and be killed. I have sworn an oath. But why have they assumed this whole burden, if I am to be killed? Do you understand me now? . . . For twenty-two years they have been living in this town which reeks like some squalid den where passing traders spend the night—a smell of cooking and cheap perfume and sour bedding. Here they live, and never utter a word of complaint. For twenty-two years my father has not set foot in Vienna, where he was born and brought up. Twenty-two years and never a journey, never a new piece of clothing, never a summer outing, because I must be made into the masterpiece that they in their weakness failed to achieve in their own lives. Sometimes when I am about to do something, my hand stops in midair. This eternal responsibility. I have even wished them dead," he said very softly.

"Yes," said Henrik.

They stayed in the town for four days. As they left, for the first time in their lives, they felt that something had come between them. As if one of them were in the other's debt. It could not be put into words.

And yet Konrad had a refuge which was closed to his friend: music. It was like a secret hide-out, where the world could not reach him. Henrik was not musical, and was content with Gypsy tunes and Viennese waltzes.

Music was not a topic in the academy, it was something regarded by both instructors and cadets as a kind of youthful sin to be tolerated and for-given. Each man has his weaknesses: one breeds dogs, no matter what the cost, another is obsessed with riding. Better than taking up cards, was the general opinion. And less dangerous than women.

But slowly the suspicion took hold of Henrik that music was not such a harmless pleasure after all. Naturally the academy did not tolerate real music, with its power to arouse and erupt into naked emotion. The curriculum certainly included musical instruction, but only in its most basic aspects.

The boys did learn that music required brass, and a drum major to march in front and throw his silver staff periodically into the air, and a pony to carry the kettledrum behind the band. That was proper music—loud, regular music that set the pace for the troops, brought the civilians out into the streets, and was the unalterable ornament of every parade. Men stepped out more smartly to music, and that was that. Sometimes it was high-spirited, sometimes pompous or solemn. Beyond that, nobody paid any attention.

But when Konrad heard music, he turned pale. Every kind of music, even the simplest, struck him like a physical blow. The color left his face, and his lips trembled. Music communicated something to him that the others could never achieve. It seemed that the melodies did not speak to the rational portion of his mind. The discipline he demanded of himself, which he accepted as both punishment and penance, and by means of which he had achieved a certain status in the world, relaxed at such moments, as if his body too were releasing itself from its rigid posture. It was like the moment on parade when "stand to attention" finally gave way to "at ease." His lips moved, as if he wanted to say something. At such times he forgot where he was, his eyes sparkled, he stared into the distance, oblivious of his surroundings, his superiors, his companions, the beautiful ladies, the rest of the audience in the theater. When he listened to music, he listened with his whole body, as longingly as a condemned man in his cell aches for the sound of distant feet perhaps bringing news of his release. When spoken to, he didn't hear. Music dissolved the world around him just as it dissolved the laws of artistic unity, and at such moments Konrad ceased to be a soldier.

One evening in summer, he was playing a four-handed piece with Henrik's mother, when something happened. It was before dinner, they were in the main reception room, the Officer of the Guards and his son were sitting in a corner listening politely, the way patient and well-intentioned people do, with an attitude of "Life is made up of duties. Music is one of them. Ladies' wishes are to be obeyed." They were performing Chopin's Polonaise-Fantaisie and Henrik's mother was playing with such passion that the whole room seemed to shimmer and vibrate. As they waited patiently and politely in their corner for the piece finally to end, both father and son had the sensation that some metamorphosis was taking place in Henrik's mother and in Konrad. It was as if the music were levitating the furniture, as if some mighty force were blowing against the heavy silk curtains, as if every ossified, decayed particle buried deep in the human heart were quickening into life, as if in everyone on earth a fatal rhythm lay dormant, waiting for the predestined moment to begin its fateful beat. The courteous listeners realized that music is dangerous. But the duo at the piano had lost all thought of danger. The Polonaise-Fantaisie was no more than a pretext to loose upon the world those forces that shake and explode the structures of order which man has devised to conceal what lies beneath. They sat straight-backed at the piano, leaning away from the keys a little and yet bound to them, as if music itself were driving an invisible team of fiery mythical horses riding the storm that circled the world, and they were bracing their bodies to maintain a firm grip on the reins in this explosive headlong gallop of unshackled energies. And then, with a single chord, they ended. The evening sun was slanting through the large windows, and motes of gold were spinning in its rays, as if the unearthly racing chariot had stirred up a whirlwind of dust on its way to ruin and the void.

"Chopin," said the French wife and mother, breathing heavily. "His father was French."

"And his mother Polish," said Konrad, turning his head sideways and looking out of the windows. "He was a relative of my mother's," he added parenthetically, as if ashamed of this connection.

They all paid attention to his words, because there was a great sadness in his voice; he sounded like an exile speaking of home and the longing to return. The Officer of the Guards bent forward as he stared at his son's friend; he seemed to be seeing him for the first time. That evening, when he and his son were alone in the smoking room, he said, "Konrad will never make a true soldier."

"Why?" asked his son, shocked.

But he knew that his father was right. The Officer of the Guards shrugged his shoulders, lit a cigar, stretched his legs toward the fireplace, and watched the curl of smoke. And then calmly, with the assurance of an expert, he said, "Because he is a different kind of man."

His father was long dead and many years had passed before the General understood what he had meant.

I

The truth, that other truth that lies buried beneath the roles, the costumes, the scenarios of life, is nonetheless never forgotten. The two boys grew to manhood together, swore their oath of allegiance to their Emperor together, and shared quarters together during their years in Vienna, for the Officer of the Guards had arranged for his son and Konrad to serve their first tour of duty in the vicinity of the Imperial court. From the deaf widow of a regimental doctor who lived near the Schönbrunn park they rented three rooms on the second floor of a narrow house with a gray façade and windows that opened onto a long, narrow, overgrown garden thick with green-gage trees. Konrad rented a piano but played only rarely; he seemed to fear music. They lived there like brothers, but Henrik sometimes had the uneasy sensation that his friend was concealing a secret.

Konrad was "another kind of man," and his secret was not one that yielded to questioning. He was always calm, always peaceable. He performed his duties, spent time with his comrades, and went out in society all as if military service were a constant, as if all of life were a single uninterrupted tour of duty, both day and night. They were young officers, and Henrik was concerned that Konrad was living like a monk. Like someone who did not belong to this world. After his hours of duty, it seemed that another duty began that was more demanding and more complicated, just as a young monk dedicates himself not only to the prayers and rituals that are his form of duty, but also to solitude, contemplation, even mystical dreams. Konrad feared music and the secret bond between them that laid claim not only to his mind but to his body; he feared that it had the power to command his fate, throw him off course and crush him. In the mornings the two friends went riding together in the Prater or in the riding school, then Konrad was on duty, after which he returned to the apartment in Hietzing; sometimes weeks went by without his making any evening engagement. The old house was still lit by oil lamps and candles; the son of the Officer of the Guards almost always returned home after midnight from a ball or an evening entertainment, and while he was still in his cab on the street he could see the despondent, reproachful glimmer of the dim flickering light. The glow in the window seemed a signal of rebuke. The son of the Officer of the Guards handed the coach-man a coin, paused in the silent street in front of the old door, took off his gloves, reached for the key, and had a faint sense that once again this evening he had betrayed his friend. He came from the world where soft music lilted through dining rooms and ball-rooms and salons, but not the way his friend liked it. It was played to make life sweeter and more festive, to make women's eyes flash and men's vanity throw sparks; that was its raison d'être throughout the city, wherever the son of the Officer of the Guards whiled away the nights of his youth. Konrad's music, on the other hand, didn't offer forgetfulness; it aroused

by

people to feelings of passion and guilt, and demanded that people be truer to themselves in heart and mind. Such music is upsetting, the son of the Officer of the Guards thought to himself, and began rebelliously to whistle a waltz. That year the fashionable composer being whistled by all Vienna was the younger Strauss. He took the key and opened the ancient gate which slowly creaked ajar, crossed the wide vestibule at the foot of the musty, vaulted stairwell lit by oil lamps in uneven glass shades, paused for a moment, and glanced out at the snow-covered garden in the moonlight, looking as if it had been filled in with a stick of white chalk between the dark outlines of things. Everything was peaceful. Vienna was sound asleep under the falling snow. The Emperor was asleep in the Hofburg and fifty million of his subjects were asleep in his lands. The son of the Officer of the Guards felt that this silence was also in part his responsibility, that he, too, was keeping watch over the sleep and safety of the Emperor and his fifty million subjects, even when he was doing no more than wearing his uniform with honor, going out in the evening, listening to waltzes, drinking French red wine, and saying to ladies and gentlemen exactly what they wished to hear from him. He felt that he obeyed a strict regime of laws, both written and unwritten, and that this obedience was also a duty which he fulfilled in the salons just as he fulfilled it in the barracks or on the drill ground. Fifty million people found their security in the feeling that their Emperor was in bed every night before midnight and up again before five, sitting by candlelight at his desk in an American rush-bottomed chair, while everyone else who had pledged their loyalty to him was obeying the customs and the laws. Naturally true obedience required a deeper commitment than that prescribed by laws. Obedience had to be rooted in the heart: that was what really counted. People had to be certain that everything was in its place. That was the year that the son of the Officer of the Guards and his friend turned twenty-two.

The two of them, young officers in Vienna. The son of the Officer of the Guards climbed the rotted stairs, whistling his waltz half under his breath. Everything in this house smelled a little musty, the stairs, the rooms, and yet it was somehow a pleasant smell, as if the interior retained a lingering odor of fruit preserves. That winter, carnival season broke out like a happy epidemic. Every evening in the white-and-gold salons there was dancing under the flickering tongues of flame in the gaslit chandeliers. Snow kept falling, and coachmen drove pairs of lovers silently through the white air. All Vienna danced in the snowflakes and every morning the son of the Officer of the Guards went to the old indoor riding ring to watch the Spanish riders and their Lippizaners going through their paces. Riders and horses shared a nobility and distinction, an almost guilty ease and rhythm inborn in soul and body. Then, because he was young, he went walking. As he sauntered past the shops in the center of the city in the company of other strollers, he would occasionally be greeted by a waiter or the driver of a hansom cab because he looked so like his father. Vienna and the monarchy made up one enormous family of Hungarians, Germans, Moravians, Czechs, Serbs, Croats, and Italians, all of whom secretly understood that the only person who could keep order among this fantastical welter of longings, impulses, and emotions was the Emperor, in his capacity of Sergeant Major and Imperial Majesty, government clerk in sleeve protectors and Grand Seigneur, unmannerly clod and absolute ruler. Vienna was in high, good mood. The stuffy high-vaulted taverns in the old city served the best beer in the world, and as the bells chimed midday the streets filled with the rich smells of goulash, spreading friendliness and goodwill as if there were eternal peace on earth. Women carried fur muffs and wore hats with feathers, and veils that they pulled down over their faces against the snow, leaving a glimpse of nose and flashing eyes. At four in the afternoon the gaslights were lit in the cafés and coffee with whipped cream was served to the generals and officials at their regular tables while, outside, blushing women shrank into the corners of hired carriages as they raced toward bachelor apartments where the log fires were already lit, for it was carnival and there was an uprising of love throughout the city, as if the agents of some giant conspiracy were goading and inflaming hearts across all levels of society.

In the hour before curtain time in the theaters, vinophiles met discreetly in the cellars of Prince Esterhazy's palace, tables were being laid for archdukes in the private rooms at the Sacher, and in the hot, smoky rooms of the wine cellar next to St.

Stephen's Cathedral, restless, unhappy Polish gentlemen drank schnapps, for things in their country were not going well. But there were hours that winter in Vienna when it seemed that everyone was happy, which was what the son of the Officer of the Guards was thinking as he contentedly whistled his half-stifled tune. In the vestibule the warmth from the tiled stove reached out to welcome him like a handshake from a trusted friend. Everything in this city was laid out so generously, and everything was in its perfect place. If the archdukes for their part were a trifle uncouth, the caretakers were the secret beneficiaries in this all-inclusive hierarchy. The servant jumped up from his place next to the stove to take his master's coat, shako, and gloves even as his other hand was reaching for the bottle of burgundy in its warming place; the son of the Officer of the Guards was in the habit of slowly sipping a glass every night before he went to bed, as if each swallow were a weighty word that distanced him from the frivolous memories of the day and the evening. The man was already following him into Konrad's dimly lit room, bearing the bottle on a silver tray.

Sometimes they sat talking there until dawn,

while the stove cooled and the son of the Officer of the Guards worked his way to the end of the bottle. Konrad talked about his reading; Henrik talked about life. Konrad couldn't afford life, for him military service was a career involving a rank, a uniform, and a wide range of the most intricate and subtle consequences. The son of the Officer of the Guards sensed that their bond of friendship, fragile and complex in the way of all significant relationships between people, must be protected from the influence of money and any slightest hint of envy or tactlessness. It was not easy. The son of the Officer of the Guards begged Konrad to accept some portion of his fortune, since he truly had no idea what to do with it. Konrad told him he could not accept so much as a filler. And both knew that this was how things must be: the son of the Officer of the Guards could not give Konrad money, and he also had to accept that he would go out in society and live a life appropriate to his rank while Konrad remained at home in Hietzing, ate scrambled eggs five nights a week, and personally tallied his underwear when it was returned from the laundry. But that was not what was important: what was much more alarming was that this friendship, despite the discrepancy in their wealth, must be protected for a lifetime.

Konrad aged quickly. At twenty-five he needed reading glasses. When his friend returned at night from Vienna and the world, smelling of tobacco and perfume, a little tipsy and in a boyish fashion a sophisticate, they talked long and quietly, like conspirators, as if Konrad were a magician sitting by the hearth ruminating on the meaning of existence, while his amanuensis busied himself out there among men, lying in wait to steal life's secrets. Konrad preferred reading English books, studies in social history and social progress. The son of the Officer of the Guards only read books about horses and great journeys. And because of their friendship, each forgave the other's original sin: wealth on the one hand and poverty on the other.

The "difference" that Henrik's father had mentioned when the Countess and Konrad were playing the Polonaise-Fantaisie gave the latter a power over the soul of his friend.

Of what did this consist? Every exercise of power incorporates a faint, almost imperceptible, element of contempt for those over whom the power is exercised. One can only dominate another human soul if one knows, understands, and with the utmost tact despises the person one is subjugating. As time went on, the nightly conversations in Hietzing took on the tone of conversations between master and pupil. Like all those compelled by inclination and external circumstances to premature solitude, Konrad's tone as he spoke of the world was gently ironic, gently disdainful, and yet in some involuntary fashion full of curiosity, as if the events that presumably took place over there on the other side were of interest only to children and those even less experienced than they. But his voice betrayed a certain homesickness: youth always yearns for that terrifying, suspect, indifferent homeland known as the world. And when Konrad amicably, jokingly, casually, condescendingly teased the son of the Officer of the Guards about his adventures in that world, one could hear in his voice the need of a thirsty man yearning to drain life dry.

They lived in this fashion in the flickering dazzle of youth, fulfilling a role that was also a profession, and that gave their lives both a sense of real tension and of inner stability. Sometimes it was a woman's hand that knocked gently, with sweet excitement, on the door of the apartment in Hietzing. One day the hand belonged to Veronika, the dancer—the memory of this name makes the General rub his eyes as if he had just been jolted awake out of a deep sleep with shreds of dreams still lingering in his head. Yes, Veronika. And then Angela, the young widow of the medical officer, who was obsessed with horse-racing. No, rather, Veronika, the dancer. She lived in the attic apartment of an ancient house in Three-Horseshoe Lane; it was a single large studio, and impossible to heat properly. But it was the only place she could live, given the space she required for her exercises and steps.

The echoing room was decorated with dusty bouquets of dried flowers and animal portraits done by a painter from Steiermark who had left them for the landlord in lieu of rent. Sheep had been his favorite subject, and it was gloomy sheep with damp, vacant, questioning eyes that stared at the visitor from all corners of the room. Veronika lived in all this while surrounded by dust-laden curtains and worn-out furniture.

As one came up the stairs, one could already

smell the strong scents she wore, attar of roses and French perfumes. One summer evening, all three of them went out to dinner together. The General remembers it well, as if he were inspecting a painting with a magnifying glass. It was in a little country tavern in the woods near Vienna. They had ridden out there in a carriage through the fragrant trees. The dancer wore a wide-brimmed hat of Florentine straw, white elbow-length crocheted gloves, a tight-fitting dress of rose silk, and black silk shoes. Even her bad taste was perfect. She teetered uncertainly across the gravel under the trees as if every footstep taken on bare ground in the direction of the tavern were unworthy of her. As one would preserve a Stradivarius from having to play mere drinking songs, she preserved the masterpieces that were her legs, dedicated as they were to the art of the dance and the suspension of earth's gravity, from the tragic limitations of the body. They ate in the courtyard of the simple tavern overgrown with wild vines by the light of candles set in glass shades. They drank a light red wine and the young woman laughed a great deal. On the way home, as they crested a hill and looked down at the city shimmering in the moonlight,

Veronika spontaneously threw her arms around their necks. It was a moment of pure happiness, pure being. Silently they accompanied the dancer to her door and kissed her hand in farewell. Veronika. And Angela with her horses. And all the others, with flowers in their hair, circling past in a dance, scattering blossoms, notes, ribbons, and long gloves in their wake. These women had brought the intoxication of love's first adventures into their lives, and with it all its companions: desire, jealousy, and the struggle with loneliness. And yet, beyond their roles and their lives in society, beyond the women, something else, something more powerful made itself felt. A feeling known only to men. A feeling called friendship.

8

The General dressed himself without summoning the servant. He took his dress uniform out of the wardrobe and gazed at it for a long time. It had been decades since he had worn it. He opened a drawer, took out his decorations, and lifted them from their boxes lined in red, white, and green silk. As he held the medals of bronze, silver, and gold in his hand and ran his fingers over them, he saw in his mind's eye a bridgehead over the Dnieper, or a parade in Vienna, or a reception in Buda's royal palace. He shrugged. What had life brought him? Duties and idle pleasures. Like a card player absentmindedly gathering up his chips after a big game, he let the decorations slide back into the drawer.

He dressed in black, tied his tie of white piqué, and ran a wet brush through his white, close-cropped hair. In the last years these austere, almost priestly clothes had become his uniform. He went to his desk, fumbled in his portfolio with trembling old fingers for a tiny key, and unlocked a long, deep drawer. From its secret compartment he removed a number of different objects: a Belgian revolver, a little packet of letters tied with blue ribbon, and a book bound in yellow velvet with the word "souvenir" imprinted on the cover. The book was also closed with a blue ribbon and the knot had been stamped with a seal. The General held it in his hand for a long time. Then he checked the weapon with expert attention. It was an old revolver with six chambers. All six had bullets in them. With a casual flick of the wrist he dropped the revolver back into the drawer, and shrugged again, then slipped the yellow-velvet-bound book deep into the pocket of his jacket.

He stepped to the windows and opened the

shutters. While he had been asleep there had been a sudden cloudburst. A cool breeze was moving between the plane trees, and the wet leaves glistened as if they had been oiled. It was already dusk. He stood motionless at the window, arms crossed over his chest, looking out at the landscape, the valley, the forest, the yellow road far below, the distant outline of the town. His farsighted eyes picked up the movement of a steadily advancing carriage. His guest was en route.

Face expressionless, body motionless, he followed the rapidly moving target. Then he closed one eye as a hunter does when taking aim.

9

It was already past seven o'clock when the General came out of his bedroom. Leaning on his ivory-headed cane, he walked with slow, measured steps down the long corridor that linked this wing of the castle, with its private quarters, to the great public rooms, the reception hall, the music room, the salons. The walls of the corridor were hung with old portraits in gold frames: portraits of ancestors, of great-grandfathers and great-grandmothers, of friends, of former servants, of regimental comrades and famous guests. It was a tradition in the General's family to employ a resident artist: sometimes itinerant painters, but sometimes also better-known men, such as the artist from Prague who had spent eight years here during the General's grandfather's time and had painted everyone who came within range of his brushes, including the majordomo and the winning racehorses. His great-grandfather and great-grandmother had fallen victim to the attentions of amateur artists indulging their wanderlust, and stared down from the wall in their robes of state. They were followed by a number of serious, composed male figures—contemporaries of the Officer of the Guards, with Hungarian moustaches and curled forelocks, wearing black formal clothes or dress uniforms. It had been a good generation, the General thought, as he looked at the portraits of his father's relatives, friends, and military comrades. A good generation, a trifle eccentric, not at ease in society, arrogant, but absolutely dedicated to honor, to the male virtues: silence, solitude, the inviolability of one's word, and women. If they were let down, they remained silent. Most of them were silent for a lifetime, bound to duty and discretion as if by vows. Toward the far end of the corridor were the

French portraits, French ladies with powdered hair, fat bewigged gentlemen with sensual lips, distant relations of his mother, unknown faces looming dimly out of their backgrounds of blue, pink, and dove gray. Then the picture of his father in his Guards' uniform. Then one of the portraits of his mother, in a feathered hat and carrying a whip like an equestrian in a circus. Then a blank space, about a meter square, with a ghostly gray line marking the perimeter where once a picture had hung. The General walked past the empty space impassively and reached the landscapes.

The nurse was standing at the end of the corridor in a black dress with a freshly starched white cap on her head.

"What are you looking at? The pictures?" she asked.

"Yes."

"Don't you want us to hang the picture back up?" she asked, pointing directly at the blank space on the wall with the bluntness of the very old.

"Is it still here?" the General asked. The nurse nodded.

"No," he said, after a short pause. Then, softer, "I

did not know you had kept it. I thought you had burned it."

"There is absolutely no sense," said the nurse in a high, thin voice, "in burning pictures."

"No," said the General candidly, the way one would talk to one's nurse and no one else. "That isn't what matters."

They turned toward the grand staircase and looked down into the outer hall, where a manservant and the chambermaid were arranging flowers in crystal vases.

In the intervening hours the castle had come to life like a device whose mechanism has been wound up and reset: not only the furniture, chairs, and sofas liberated from their linen shrouds, but also the paintings on the walls, the enormous wrought-iron chandeliers, the ornaments in their glass cabinets and on the mantelpieces. Logs were piled in the hearth ready for a fire, for it was the end of summer and after midnight the cold mist spread a damp breath through the rooms. All of a sudden the objects seemed to take on meaning, as if to prove that everything in the world acquires significance only in relation to human activity and human destiny.

They regarded the outer hall, the flowers on the table which had been set down in front of the fireplace, and the arrangement of the armchairs.

"That leather chair stood on the right," he said.

"You remember so clearly?" asked the nurse, her eyes blinking.

"Yes," he said. "Konrad sat there in it under the clock, by the fire. I sat in the middle, facing the fire, in the Florentine chair, and Krisztina opposite, in the armchair my mother brought with her."

"You're so exact," said the nurse.

"Yes." The General leaned against the banisters, looking down. "In the blue crystal vase there were dahlias. Forty-one years ago."

"You certainly remember." The nurse sighed.

"I remember," he said calmly. "Is the table laid with the French porcelain?"

"Yes, the flowered service," said Nini.

"Good." He nodded, reassured. Now for a time they both stood silently observing the scene that was displayed before them, the great reception room below, the imposing pieces of furniture which had been guarding a memory, a fateful hour, or even a moment, as if until one particular second these dead objects had had no existence beyond the physical properties of wood, metal, and cloth, and then, suddenly, on a single evening forty-one years ago, they had been filled with life and meaning and had acquired a totally new significance. And now, as they sprang to life again like freshly wound automata, these objects were remembering.

"What will you serve our guest?"

"Trout," said Nini. "Soup and trout. A cut of beef and salad. A guinea-fowl. And a flambéed ice. The cook hasn't made it for more than ten years. But perhaps it will be good," she said, worried.

"Make sure it turns out well. Last time there were also crayfish," he said quietly, apparently directing his words downstairs.

"Yes," said the nurse calmly. "Krisztina liked crayfish, no matter how they were prepared. There were still crayfish in the stream back then. But not anymore. And I cannot send to town for them at this time of night."

"Pay attention to the wine," the General murmured conspiratorially. The nurse instinctively moved closer and bent her head to hear better, in the intimate way that only longtime servants and family members do. "Have the '86 Pommard brought up from the cellar, and some of the Chablis for the fish. And a bottle of the old Mumm, a magnum. Do you remember?"

"Yes." The nurse thought for a moment. "But all we have left is the brut. Krisztina drank the demi-sec."

"One mouthful. Always one mouthful with the roast. She didn't care for champagne."

"What do you want from this man?" asked the nurse.

"The truth," said the General.

"You know it perfectly well."

"I do not know it," he said loudly, untroubled by the fact that the manservant and the chambermaid stopped arranging the flowers and looked up at him. But then they glanced back down and their hands set to work again automatically.

"The truth is precisely what I don't know."

"But you know the facts," said the nurse sharply.

"Facts are not the truth," retorted the General. "Facts are only one part of it. Not even Krisztina knew the truth. Perhaps Konrad. . . . And now I am going to get it from him," he said calmly.

"What are you going to get from him?"

"The truth," he said abruptly, and then was silent.

When the manservant and the chambermaid had left the hall and they were alone up above, the nurse, too, leaned her forearms against the banisters, as if the two of them were standing on a mountain-top admiring the view. Speaking the words down into the room where three people had sat once in front of the fire, she said, "There is something I must tell you. When Krisztina was dying, she called for you."

"Yes," said the General. "I was there."

"You were there and yet you weren't there. You were so far away you might as well have been on a voyage. You were in your room, and she was dying. Alone with me, round about dawn. And then she asked for you. I am telling you this because you should know it this evening."

The General said nothing.

"I think he has arrived." He straightened up. "Take care of the wines and keep an eye on every-thing else, Nini."

There was the sound of gravel crunching in the

driveway, followed by the rumble of wheels outside the doors. The General leaned his stick against the banisters and began to descend the staircase to meet his guest. He paused for a moment near the top. "The candles," he said. "Do you remember? . . . The blue candles for the table. Do we still have them? Light them before we sit down, they should be burning during dinner."

"I hadn't remembered," said the nurse.

"But I did," he replied argumentatively.

Solemnly and in elderly dignity, he walked down the staircase, his back ramrod straight in his black evening clothes. The great glass door to the reception hall swung open, and there behind the man-servant was an old man.

"You see, I have come back again," the guest said softly.

"I never doubted that you would," replied the General, as softly, and smiled.

They shook hands with great formality.

10

They walked over to the fireplace and in the cold glow cast by the wall lights they subjected each other, in the blink of an eye, to a sharp and expert appraisal.

Konrad was a few months older than the General; he had turned seventy-five in the spring. The two old men looked at each other with the knowledge that only the aged can bring to the vagaries of the body: with an absolute attention to physical evidence, seeking the remaining signs of vital energy, the faint traces of joie de vivre still illuminating their faces and energizing their bearing.

"No," said Konrad seriously. "Neither of us is getting any younger."

Yet both of them experienced the same flash of envious but joyful surprise as they recognized that the other had passed the hard test: the forty-one years that had elapsed, the time of their separation in which they had not seen each other and yet had known of each other at every hour, had not broken them. We endured, thought the General. And his guest felt a strange sensation of peace, mingled with both disappointment and pleasure—disappointment, because the other man was standing there alert and healthy, pleasure because he himself had managed to return here in full possession of his powers—as he thought, "He's been waiting for me, and that's what's kept him strong."

It was a feeling that communicated itself to them both just then: that during all these decades they had drawn their strength from waiting itself, as if an entire life had been mere preparation for a single task.

Konrad had known that one day he would have to come back, just as the General had known that someday this moment would arrive. It was what both had lived for.

Konrad was as pale as he had been in his youth, and it was evident that he still led an indoor life and avoided fresh air. He, too, was wearing dark clothes of sober but very fine material.

He must be rich, thought the General. They looked at each other for a long moment without speaking. Then the manservant came with absinthe and schnapps.

"Where have you come from?" asked the General.

"From London."

"Do you live there?"

"Close by. I have a small house near London. When I came back from the tropics I settled there."

"Where in the tropics?"

"In Singapore." He lifted a pale hand and pointed vaguely to a spot in the air as if to locate the place in the universe where he had once lived. "But only at the end. Before that, I was far inland on the peninsula, with the Malays."

"They say," said the General, raising his glass of absinthe to the light in the gesture of a welcoming toast, "that the tropics use people up and make them old."

"They're terrible," said Konrad. "They take ten years off a man's life."

"But it doesn't show. Welcome!"

They emptied their glasses and sat down.

"Really not?" asked the guest as he settled himself in the armchair beside the fire, under the clock. The General watched his movements with care. Now that his friend had chosen to sit in the armchair—exactly where he had last sat forty-one years ago, as if he were involuntarily obeying the local magic—the General blinked in relief. He felt the way a hunter feels when he finally sees the game in the position it has been carefully avoiding. Now everything had fallen into place.

"The tropics are terrible," Konrad said again. "People like us cannot tolerate them. They use up the body and destroy the constitution. They kill some part of you."

"Is that why you went?" asked the General almost as an aside, giving no particular emphasis to the words. "To kill something in yourself?"

His tone was polite and conversational, and he took his seat facing the fireplace in the old armchair known in the family as the "Florentine Chair," where he had sat in the evenings forty-one years ago talking with Krisztina and Konrad. Now the two of them glanced at the third chair, upholstered in French silk, and empty.

"Yes," said Konrad calmly.

"And were you successful?"

"I am already old," said Konrad, looking into the fire, not answering the question.

They both sat in silence, watching the flames, until the manservant came to announce dinner.

11

"It's like this," said Konrad after the trout. "At first you think you can get used to it." He was speaking of the tropics. "I was still young when I arrived, thirty-two, you remember. I went straight out into the swamps. You live out there in little huts with tin roofs. I had no money—everything was paid by the Colonial Company. At night you lie in bed and it is like lying in a warm mist. By day the mist is thicker and scalding hot. Soon you become quite apathetic. Everyone drinks, everyone's eyes are bloodshot. In the first year, you think you will die. In the third year, you realize that you are no longer the person you were, and that the rhythm of life has changed. You live faster, something inside you burns, your heart beats differently and at the same time, you become indifferent to everything. Absolutely everything, for months at a time. Then there comes a moment when you no longer have any idea what is happening either inside you or around you. Sometimes that takes five years, sometimes it happens in the first few months. That's when the rage comes. A lot of people become murderous, others kill themselves."

"Even the English?"

"Less often. But even they get infected with this fever of rage, as if it were a bacillus, though it isn't. And yet I'm convinced it is a form of illness. It's just that no one has found the cause yet. Maybe it comes from the water. Or the plants. Or love affairs. You cannot get used to Malaysian women. Some of them are extraordinarily beautiful. They smile, their skin is so smooth, their bodies are so supple when they serve you at table or in bed . . . and yet you cannot get used to them. The English know how to defend themselves. They arrive with England in their suitcases. Their courteous arrogance. Their reserve.

Their golf courses and their tennis courts. Their whisky. Their evening dress, that they change into every night in their tin-roofed houses out in the middle of the swamps. Not all of them, of course. That's just a legend. Most of them turn brutal after four or five years just like the others, the Belgians, the French, the Dutch. The tropics eat away their college manners the way leprosy eats away skin. Oxford and Cambridge rot down. Back home in the British Isles, everyone who has spent time in the tropics is suspect. They may be respected and honored, but they are also suspect. I'm convinced that their entries in the security files are annotated with the word 'tropics,' the way others would be stamped 'blood disease' or 'spying.' Everyone who has spent extended time in the tropics is suspect, no matter whether they've played golf and tennis, drunk whisky in the clubs in Singapore, appeared at the Governor's receptions in evening dress or in uniform and decorations, they're still suspect. Because they have experienced the tropics. Because they carry this alarming contagious disease, and there's no known defense against it, and yet it's somehow both deadly and seductive. The tropics are a disease. Tropical diseases have a cure, but the tropics themselves do not."

"I understand," said the General. "Did you catch it too?"

"Everyone does." The guest savored the Chablis with his head tilted back, tasting it in small mouthfuls like a connoisseur. "To become an alcoholic is to get off lightly. Passions swirl out there like the tornados in the forests and mountains beyond the swamps. All sorts of passions. Which is why the English are suspicious of everyone who comes back from the tropics. Nobody knows what's in their blood or their nerves or their hearts. What's certain is that they're no longer Europeans. Not quite. They may have had the European newspapers delivered by mail, they may have read everything that has been thought and read in this part of the world for the last decades and longer, they may have maintained all the strange formalities that whites in the tropics observe among themselves the way drunkards conduct themselves with excessive precision in society: they hold themselves too strictly, so that nobody will detect their chaotic feelings, they're as smooth as eels and utterly correct and perfectly mannered . . . and inside everything looks different."

96

"Really?" said the General, holding his glass of white wine to the light. "Tell me what's inside." And when the other said nothing, "I think you came here this evening to tell me."

They are sitting at the long table in the great dining room where no guest has sat since Krisztina's death, where no one has eaten for decades, and the room is like a museum of furniture and household objects from a bygone era. The walls are covered with old French paneling, the furniture is from Versailles. They sit at either end of the long table, separated by crystal vases of orchids in the center of the damask cloth. Interspersed with the arrangement of flowers are four porcelain figures of the finest Sèvres: exquisitely charming allegories of North, South, East, and West. West is pointing toward the General, while Konrad's figure is the East, a grinning little saracen with a palm tree and a camel.

A row of porcelain candlesticks stands the length of the table, holding thick, blue religious candles. The only other light comes from hidden points in the four corners of the room. The candles burn high with a flickering light in the surrounding dimness.

Logs glow darkly in the gray marble fireplace. The French doors stand open a little, the gray silk curtains are not quite closed, and the summer evening breezes come through the windows from time to time, while the thin curtains reveal the moonlit landscape and the glimmering lights of the little town in the distance.

At the midpoint of the long table with its flowers and candles is another chair, covered in Gobelin tapestry work, its back to the fireplace. It was where Krisztina, the General's wife, sat. Where the place setting should be is the allegorical figure of the South: a lion, with an elephant and a black-skinned man in a burnous, all occupying a space no bigger than a side plate and keeping watch over something in companionable harmony. The majordomo in his black frock coat stands motionless in the background, keeping watch over the serving table and directing the servants—dressed tonight in knee breeches and black tailcoats in the French manner— simply by moving his eyes. The General's mother was the one who had established French customs here as the order of the household, and whenever she ate in this room—whose furniture, plates, gold cutlery, glasses, crystal vases, and paneling had all come with her from her foreign homeland—she had always insisted that the servants dress and serve accordingly. It is so quiet in the room that even the faint crackling of the logs is audible. The two men are speaking in hushed tones and yet their voices echo: like stringed instruments, the ancient wooden panels covering the walls also vibrate to the muffled words, amplifying them.

"No," says Konrad, who has been thinking as he was eating. "I came because I was in Vienna."

He eats quickly, with neat movements but the greediness of old age. Now he lays down his fork, bends forward a little and raises his voice as he almost calls down the table to his host sitting far away at the other end: "I came because I wanted to see you one more time. Isn't it natural?"

"Nothing could be more natural," the General replies courteously. "So you were in Vienna. After the tropics and their passions, it must have been a great experience. Is it a long time since you were last there?"

He asks politely, without a trace of irony in his voice. The guest looks at him distrustfully from the other end of the table. They sit there a little lost, the two old men in the large room, so far from each other.

"Yes, a long time," Konrad replies. "Forty years. It was when . . ." He speaks uncertainly, stumbling involuntarily in his embarrassment. "It was when I was on my way to Singapore."

"I understand," says the General. "And this time, what did you find in Vienna?"

"Change," says Konrad. "At my age and in my circumstances, all one encounters wherever one goes is change. Admittedly, I did not set foot on the continent of Europe for forty years. I only spent the occasional hour in one French port or another en route from Singapore to London. But I wanted to see Vienna again. And this house."

"Is that why you made the trip?" asks the General. "To see Vienna and this house? Or do you have business on the Continent?"

"I am no longer active in any way whatever," Konrad answers. "Like you, I'm seventy-five years old. I shall die soon. That's why I made the trip. That's why I'm here."

"They say," says the General politely and encouragingly, "that when one reaches our age, one lives until one is tired of it. Don't you find?"

"I'm tired of it already," says the guest. His voice is composed, uninflected. "Vienna," he says. "To me it was the tuning fork for the entire world. Saying the word Vienna was like striking a tuning fork and then listening to find out what tone it called forth in the person I was talking to. It was how I tested people. If there was no response, this was not the kind of person I liked.

"Vienna wasn't just a city, it was a tone that either one carries forever in one's soul or one does not. It was the most beautiful thing in my life. I was poor, but I was not alone, because I had a friend. And Vienna was like another friend. When it rained in the tropics, I always heard the voice of Vienna. And at other times too. Sometimes deep in the virgin forests I smelled the musty smell of the entrance hall in the house in Hietzing. Music and everything I loved was in the stones of Vienna, and in people's glances and their behavior, the way pure feelings are part of one's very heart. You know when the feelings stop hurting. Vienna in winter and spring. The allées in Schönbrunn. The blue light in the dormitory at the academy, the great white stair-well with the baroque statue. Mornings riding in the Prater. The mildew in the riding school. I remember all of it exactly, and I wanted to see it again," he says softly, almost ashamed.

"And after forty-one years, what did you find?" the General asks again.

"A city," says Konrad with a shrug. "Change."

"Here at least," says the General, "you won't be disappointed. Almost nothing has changed here."

"Did you ever travel in recent years?"

"Rarely." The General stares into the candle flame. "Only on military duty. For a time, I thought of resigning my commission, like you, and traveling out in the world to look around and find something or someone."

They do not look at each other: the guest fixes his eyes on the golden liquid in his glass, the General on the candle flame. "And then finally I stayed here. One's military service, you know. One becomes rigid, obdurate. I promised my father I would serve out my time. That's why I stayed. Though I did take early retirement. When I was fifty, they wanted to put me in charge of an army. I felt I was too young for that, so I resigned. They understood. Besides," he gestures to the servant to pour the red wine, "it was a time when military service offered no satisfaction anymore. The revolution. The end of the monarchy."

"Yes," says the guest. "I've heard about that."

"Only heard about it? We lived through it," says the General severely.

"Perhaps a little more," the other says now. "It was in '17. I was back in the tropics for the second time. I was working out in the swamplands with Chinese and Malay coolies. The Chinese are the best. They gamble away everything they've got, but they're the best. We were living in virgin forest in the middle of the swamps. No telephone. No radio. War was raging in the world outside. I was already a British citizen, but the authorities were very understanding: I could not fight against my former homeland. They comprehend such things. Which was why I was allowed to return to the tropics. Out there, we knew absolutely nothing, the coolies least of all. Yet, one day, in the middle of the swamps, minus newspapers or radio, several weeks' journey away from all sources of news from the wider world, they stopped work. At twelve noon. Without any reason whatever. Nothing around them had changed, not the conditions of their work nor the discipline nor their provisions. None of it was particularly good or bad, it all depended on circumstances, the way it always did out there. And one day in '17 at twelve noon, they announce that they're not going to work any more. They came out of the jungle, four thousand coolies, mud up to their hips, naked to the waist, laid down their tools, their axes, and mattocks, and said: Enough. And made this and that demand. The landowners should no longer have disciplinary authority. They wanted more money. Longer rest periods. It was absolutely impossible to know what had got into them. Four thousand coolies transformed themselves before my very eyes into four thousand yellow and brown devils. That afternoon, I rode for Singapore. That was where I heard it. I was one of the first on the whole peninsula to get the news."

"What news?" asked the General, leaning forward.

"The news that revolution had broken out in Russia. A man called Lenin, which is all that anyone knew about him, had gone back to Russia in a sealed train, taking bolshevism in his luggage. The news reached London the same day it reached my coolies in the middle of a primeval forest without any radio or telephone. It was incomprehensible. But then I understood. People don't need machines to learn what is important to them."

"Do you think?" asked the General.

"I know," the other replies. Then, without a pause, "When did Krisztina die?"

"How did you know about Krisztina's death?" the General asks tonelessly. "You've been living in the tropics, you haven't set foot on the Continent for forty-one years. Did you sense it, the way your coolies sensed the Revolution?"

"Did I sense it? Perhaps. But she's not sitting here with us. Where else could she be, except in her grave?"

"Yes," said the General. "She's buried in the park, not far from the hothouses, in a spot she chose."

"Did she die a long time ago?"

"Eight years after you went away."

"Eight years," says the guest, and his pale lips move and his false teeth close as though he were chewing, or counting. "That's thirty-three years ago." Now he's counting half under his breath. "If she were still alive, she'd be sixty-three."

"Yes, she'd be an old woman, just as we've become old men."

"Of what did she die?"

"Anemia. A quite rare form of the disease."

"Not as rare as all that," says Konrad in a professional tone of voice. "It's quite common in the tropics. Living conditions change and the composition of the blood changes accordingly."

"It's possible," says the General. "Possible that it's relatively common in Europe, too, if living conditions change. I don't know anything about these things."

"Nor I. It's just that the tropics produce unending physical problems. Everyone becomes something of a quack doctor. Even the Malays play quack healer all the time. So she died in 1907," he says finally, as if he had been preoccupied with the arithmetic all this time and had finally figured it out. "Were you still in uniform then?"

"Yes, I served for the whole duration of the war."

"What was it like?"

"The war?" The General's expression is stiff. "As

horrifying as the tropics. The last winter in particular, up in the north. Life is adventurous here in Europe, too." He smiles.

"Adventurous? . . . Yes, I would suppose so." The guest nods in agreement. "As you may imagine, I sometimes found it very hard to bear that I wasn't back here while you were fighting. I thought of coming home and rejoining the regiment."

"That thought," says the General calmly and politely, but with a certain emphasis, "also occurred to a number of people in the regiment. But you didn't come. You must have had other things to do," he says encouragingly.

"I was an English citizen," says Konrad, embarrassed. "One cannot keep changing one's nationality every ten years."

"No." The General nods in agreement. "In my opinion, one cannot change one's nationality at all. All that can be changed are one's documents, don't you think?"

"My homeland," says the guest, "no longer exists. My homeland was Poland, Vienna, this house, the barracks in the city, Galicia, and Chopin. What's left? Whatever mysterious substance held it all together no longer works. Everything's come apart. My homeland was a feeling, and that feeling was mortally wounded. When that happens, the only thing to do is go away. Into the tropics or even further."

"Even further? Where?" asks the General coldly.

"Into time."

"This wine," says the General, lifting his glass and admiring the deep red of its contents, "is from a year you may remember. Eighty-six, the year we swore our oath to the Emperor and King. To commemorate the day, my father laid down this wine in one section of the cellar. That was many years ago, almost an entire lifetime. It's an old vintage now."

"What we swore to uphold no longer exists," says the guest very seriously as he, too, raises his glass. "Everyone has died, or gone away, or abandoned the things we swore to uphold. There was a world for which it was worth living and dying. That world is dead. The new one means nothing to me. That's all I can say."

"For me, that world is still alive, even if in reality it no longer exists. It lives, because I swore an oath to uphold it. That's all I can say."

"Yes, you are still a soldier," replies the guest.

Each at his end of the table, they raise their glasses in silence and drain them.

12

"After you went away," says the General amicably, as if the essentials, the dangerously loaded subjects, had now been disposed of and the two men were simply chatting, "we kept believing you would come back. Everybody here was waiting for you. Everybody was your friend. You were, if you will permit me, an eccentric. We forgave you because we knew that music was all-important to you. We didn't understand why you went away, but we came to terms with it, because you must have had good reason. We knew that everything was harder for you than it was for us real soldiers. What for you was a situation, for us was our calling. What for you was a disguise, for us was our fate. We were not surprised when you threw off the disguise. But we thought you would come back. Or write. A number of us thought that, myself included, I must admit. And Krisztina. And a number of people in the regiment, in case you remember."

"Only vaguely," says the guest indifferently.

"Yes, you certainly experienced a great deal in the world out there. But it's quickly forgotten."

"No," is the reply. "The world doesn't count. One never forgets what is important. I learned that only later, when I was somewhat older. Nothing secondary remains—it gets thrown away along with one's dreams. I have no memory of the regiment," he says stubbornly. "For some time now all I remember is the essentials."

"For example Vienna and this house, is that what you mean? . . ."

"Vienna and this house," the guest echoes mechanically. He stares straight ahead with eyes half-closed, blinking. "Memory has a wonderful way of separating the wheat from the chaff. There can be some great event, and ten, twenty years later one realizes that it had no effect on one whatsoever. And then one day, one remembers a hunt or a passage in a book or this room. Last time we sat here, there were three of us. Krisztina was alive. She sat there in that chair. These ornaments were on the table, too."

"Yes," says the General. "East was in front of you, South was in front of Krisztina, and West was in front of me."

"You remember it down to the details?" asks the guest, astonished.

"I remember everything."

"Sometimes the details are extremely important. They link everything together into a whole, and bind all the ingredients of memory. I used to think about that sometimes in the tropics, when it rained. That rain!" he says, as if to change the subject. "For months on end, drumming on the tin roof like a machine gun. Steam comes up off the swamps and the rain is warm. Everything is damp, the bed-clothes, your underwear, your books, the tobacco in its tin, the bread. Everything feels sticky and greasy. You're in your house, the Malays are singing. The woman you've taken to live with you sits motionless in a corner of the room and watches you. They can sit for hours like that, staring. At first you pay no attention. Then you start to feel nervous, and order them out of the room. But it doesn't help: They go and sit somewhere else, you know, in another room and stare at you through the partitions. They have huge brown eyes like those Tibetan dogs, the ones that don't bark, the most subservient animals in the whole world. They look at you with those brilliant, quiet eyes, and no matter where you go, you feel that look pursuing you like some noxious ray. Scream at her and she smiles. Strike her and she smiles. Banish her and she sits on the threshold and looks in until she is called back. They are constantly having children, though nobody ever mentions this, least of all they themselves. It is as if you are sharing quarters with an animal, a murderess, a priestess, a magician and a fanatic all rolled into one. Over time it becomes exhausting; that look is so powerful that it wears down even the strongest man. It is as powerful as the touch of a hand, as if you were constantly being stroked. It drives you mad. Then that, too, begins to leave you indifferent. It rains. You sit in your room, drink one schnapps after another, and smoke sweet tobacco. Sometimes a visitor comes, drinks schnapps, and smokes sweet tobacco. You would like to read, but somehow the rain gets into the book, too; not literally, and yet it really does, the letters are meaningless, and all you hear is the rain. You would like to play the piano, but the rain comes to sit alongside and play an accompaniment. And then dry weather returns, which is to say there is steam and bright light. People age quickly."

"In the tropics," asks the General politely, "did you sometimes play the Polonaise-Fantaisie?" They are now eating the beef, savoring it with real appetite, concentrating as they chew in the way of old people for whom eating is no longer merely the ingestion of nourishment but has become a ceremonial and archaic ritual.

They chew and swallow as if deliberately gathering strength, because strength is essential if they are to act, and strength can be drawn from rare-roasted meat and rich, dark wine. Their jaws work audibly and with absolute purpose, as if table manners have ceased to count and what matters is to masticate every shred of beef, draw out its store of energy and put it to use. Their gestures may be elegant, but they eat like tribal elders at a feast: unstoppably and without restraint.

From his corner the majordomo keeps an anxious eye on one of the servants who is in the act of using both hands to balance a large tray laden with chocolate ice cream wreathed in a tongue of bluish-yellow flame from the ignited alcohol.

The other servants pour champagne for the guest and his host. The two old men sniff the wine knowledgeably as it pours from the great bottle that is almost as large as a baby.

The General tastes it, then pushes his glass away and signals that he would like more red wine. The guest watches the gesture, blinking a little. Both men are flushed from all the food and drink.

"In my grandfather's day," says the General, looking at the wine, "a quart of ordinary wine was set in front of every guest as his individual portion. Ordinary table wine. My father told me that even the King had his guests served with crystal carafes of ordinary table wine, one each. It was called table wine because it stood on the table and each guest could drink as much as he wanted. Vintage wines were served separately. That was how wines were served at court."

"Yes," says Konrad, his face flushed, busy digesting. "Everything was well ordered in those days," he adds blandly.

"He sat here," says the General as if in passing, his eyes indicating the King's place at the center of the table. "My mother to his right, the priest to his left. He sat in this room in the place of honor. He slept upstairs in the yellow bedroom. And after dinner he danced with my mother," he says softly, his voice passing through old age and back to second childhood as he remembers. "Do you see, there's no one with whom one can talk about such things anymore. Which is another reason that I'm glad you came back," he says with utter sincerity. "Once you played the Polonaise-Fantaisie with my mother. Did you not play it again, later, in the tropics?" he asks again, as if he had just remembered what was really important.

The guest thinks for a moment. "No. I never played Chopin in the tropics. You know, this music sets loose a lot of things in me. The tropics make one more vulnerable."

Now that they have eaten and drunk, the formality and uneasiness of the first half-hour have dissipated. The blood flows hotter in their hardened arteries, and the veins stand out on their temples and foreheads. The servants bring fruit from the hothouse. They eat grapes and medlars. The room has warmed up, and the evening breezes ruffle the gray curtains at the half-open windows.

"We could have our coffee on the other side," says the General.

At that moment a violent gust of wind pushes open the windows, the curtains begin to blow, and even the heavy crystal chandelier starts swaying as if it is in a ship in a storm. The sky lights up for a moment and a sulfurous yellow bolt of lightning slices down through the night like a golden dagger impaling the body of the sacrifice. The storm is already loose in the room, extinguishing the frantic flames of the candles; suddenly it is dark. The major-domo hurries to the window and, groping in the blackness with the help of two servants, finds and closes both wings of the French doors. Then they see that the town, too, has gone dark.

The lightning has struck the municipal electric station. They sit in silence in the dark, the only light coming from the fireplace and two candles which have not blown out. Then the servants arrive with more lights.

"The other side," the General repeats, quite untroubled by either the lightning or the darkness.

A servant lifts a candelabra and leads the way. Silently, wobbling a little like shadows on a wall, they walk in this ghostly glow from the dining room through one cold salon after another until they reach a room whose only furniture consists of a grand piano with its lid raised and three chairs around a great-bellied, hot porcelain stove. They sit down and look out through the long, white curtains at the dark landscape. The servant sets the coffee on a small table along with cigars and brandy, then places the silver candelabra with the fat church candles on the ledge of the stove. They each light a cigar, and sit in silence warming themselves. The heat from the logs in the stove pours out in steady waves and the candlelight dances above their heads. The door has been closed. They are alone.

13

"We don't have long to live," the General says abruptly, as if he were pronouncing the clinching statement in an unvoiced argument. "Another year, maybe two, perhaps not even that much. We don't have long to live, because you came back. As you are well aware. You had plenty of time to think, in the tropics and then in your house near London. Forty-one years is a long time. You thought it all over, didn't you? . . . But then you came back, because you couldn't do anything else. And I've been waiting for you, because I couldn't do anything else. And we've both known that we would meet again, and then it would be all over with life and everything that gave our existence meaning and tension. A secret of the kind that lurks between the two of us has extraordinary power. It burns through the fabric of life like a scorching beam, and yet at the same time it also gives it tensile strength. It forces us to live. . . . For as long as we still have things to do here on earth, we'll stay alive. I am going to tell you what I went through, alone in this forest for forty-one years while you were out in the world and the tropics. Solitude is very strange too . . . and sometimes as filled with dangers and surprises as a virgin forest. I know all its ways. The boredom against which you mount a hopeless struggle by means of an ordered life. The sudden moments of revolt. Solitude is as full of secrets as the jungle," he repeats stubbornly. "You live a perfectly ordered existence, and one day you run amok, like those Malays of yours. You have a house, a title and a rank, and a way of life that is painfully exact. And one day you run away from it all with a weapon in your hand, or not—which may be even more dangerous. You run out into the world, wild-eyed, and your old friends and comrades get out of your way. You go to a city, you buy yourself women, everything around you turns to chaos, you look for fights everywhere and you find them. And, as I said, that is by no means the worst of it. Maybe you are struck down as you run like a mangy, rabid dog. Maybe you run full-tilt into a wall, against all life's obstacles, and break every bone in your body. What's even worse is if you take this upsurge of feeling, which has accumulated in your heart over so many lonely years, and you push it back inside. And you don't run. And you don't kill anyone. And what do you do instead? You live, you maintain discipline. You live like a monk of some heathen worldly order. But it's easy for a real monk, because he has his belief. A man who has signed away his soul and his fate to solitude is incapable of faith. He can only wait. For the day or the hour when he can talk about everything that forced him into solitude with the man or men who forced him into that condition. He prepares himself for that moment for ten or forty or forty-one years the way one prepares for a duel. He brings his affairs into order in case he dies in the duel. And he practices every day, as professional duelists do. And what weapon does he practice with? With his memories, so that he will not allow solitude and time to cloud his sight and weaken his heart and his soul. There is one duel in life, fought without sabers, that nonetheless is worth preparing for with all one's strength. And it is the most dangerous. And one day the moment comes. What do you think?" he asks courteously.

"I quite agree," says the guest, and looks at the ash of his cigar.

"I'm so glad you take the same view," says the General. "The anticipation keeps one alive. Of course, it, too, has its limits, like everything in life. If I hadn't known that you would come back one day, I would have probably set out myself to find you, in your house near London or in the tropics or in the bowels of hell. You know I would have come looking for you. Clearly one knows everything of real importance, and—you're right—one knows it without benefit of radio or telephone. Here in my house I have no telephone, only the steward has one down in the office, nor do I have a radio, as I have forbidden any of the stupid, sordid daily noise of the outside world in the rooms where I make my home.

"The world holds no further threat for me. Some

new world order may remove the way of life into which I was born and in which I have lived, forces of aggression may foment some revolution that will take both my freedom and my life. None of it matters. What matters is that I do not make any compromises with a world that I have judged and banished from my existence. Without the aid of any modern appliances, I knew that one day you would come to me again. I waited you out, because everything that is worth waiting for has its own season and its own logic. And now the moment has come."

"What do you mean by that?" asked Konrad. "I went away, which was my right. And it might be said I also had just cause. It is true that I went away without forewarning and without farewell. But I am sure you sensed and understood that I had no choice, and that it was the right thing to do."

"That you had no choice?" says the General, glancing up. His eyes are blade-sharp and they reduce his guest to the status of an object. "That is the heart of the matter. I have been breaking my head over it for a considerable time now. Forty-one years in fact, if I am not mistaken."

And, because the other man remains silent, "Now

that I am old, I spend a lot of time thinking about my childhood. Apparently this is normal. One remembers the beginning more clearly, the closer one comes to the end. I see faces and I hear voices. I see the moment when I introduced you to my father in the garden of the academy. Because you were my friend, he accepted you as his. He was not a man who was quick to accept someone as a friend, but once he gave his word, it was for life. Do you remember that moment? We were standing under the chestnut tree at the great entrance, and my father gave you his hand. 'You are my son's friend,' he said. 'You must both honor this friendship,' he added earnestly. I think nothing in life was as important to him as this. Are you listening to me? . . . Thank you. I want to tell you what happened, and to make sure I get it all in the correct order. Please do not worry, the carriage is waiting and will take you back to town whenever you would care to leave. And do not be concerned that you might have to sleep here even if you don't wish it. I could imagine that this might be uncomfortable for you. But of course if you would care to do so, you can spend the night," he adds. And as the other makes a gesture of refusal: "As you wish. The carriage is outside. It will take you back to town and in the morning you can set off for your house near London, or the tropics, or wherever you choose. But before then I ask you to listen to me."

"I am listening," says the guest.

"Good," answers the General in a lighter tone of voice. "We could also talk of other things. Two old friends on whom the sun is setting have much to remember. However, since you are here, let us speak only of the truth. So: I have begun by reminding you that my father accepted you as his friend. You know exactly what that signified to him, you knew then that any person to whom he had given his hand could count on him, no matter what blows of fate, or suffering, or need, life brought. He did not often give his hand, it is true, but once done it was without any reservation. That was how he gave you his hand in the courtyard of the academy under the chestnut trees. We were twelve years old, and it was the last moment of our childhood. Sometimes at night I see him with absolute clarity, the way I see everything really important. To my father, friendship meant the same as honor. You knew that, because you knew him. And allow me to tell you that it may have meant even more to me. Forgive me if what I am telling you makes you uncomfortable," he says softly, almost affectionately.

"I am not uncomfortable," says Konrad, just as softly. "Tell me."

"It would be good to know," the General says, as if debating with himself, "whether such a thing as friendship actually exists. I do not mean the opportunistic pleasure that two people experience in encountering each other when they think the same way about certain things at certain moments of their lives, when they share the same tasks or the same needs. None of that is friendship. Sometimes I almost believe it is the most powerful bond in life and consequently the rarest. What is its basis? Sympathy? A hollow, empty word, too weak to express the idea that in the worst times two people will stand up for each other. Or perhaps it's something else . . . perhaps buried deep in every relationship between two people is some tiny spark of erotic attraction. Here alone in the forest, trying to make sense of life, I thought about that now and then. Friendship, of course, is quite different from the affairs of those driven by morbid impulses to satisfy themselves in some fashion with others of the same sex. The eros of friendship has no need of the body. . . . That would be more of a disturbance than an arousal. And yet, it is eros all the same. Eros is present in love just as it is present in every mutual relationship. You know, I have done a great deal of reading," he says, as if to excuse himself. "These days such things are written about much more freely. But I have also repeatedly re-read Plato, because in school I wasn't yet ready to understand him. Friendship, I thought —and you who have seen the world certainly know this better than I do alone here in my village—is the noblest relationship that can exist between human beings. And it is interesting that it also exists among animals. Animals are capable of friendship, selfless-ness, and the desire to help others.

"A Russian prince—I've forgotten his name—has written about it. Lions, grouse, all sorts of creatures of every species have apparently come to the aid of others of their breed in trouble, and I've seen this for myself even when the animals are completely unre-lated. Did you ever witness something of the kind on your travels? . . . Friendship out there must surely be different, more advanced, more contemporary than it is here in our backward world. Kindred species organize mutual assistance. . . . Occasionally they have to struggle desperately against the obstacles they encounter, but there are always strong members in every community, well disposed to help. The animal world has shown me hundreds of such examples. Not so the human world. I have seen sympathy build between people, but it has always foundered in a morass of vanity and egoism. Sometimes camaraderie and fellowship look like friendship; common interests can bring about relationships akin to friendship, and in an attempt to escape loneliness, people are only too happy to involve themselves in confidences that they will later regret, but that temporarily may appear to be a variety of friendship. None of it is genuine. It is far more the case—my father knew it to be so—that friendship is a duty.

"Like the lover, the friend expects no reward for his feelings. He does not wish the performance of any duty in return, he does not view the person he has chosen as his friend with any illusion, he sees his faults and accepts him with all their consequences. Such is the ideal. And without such an ideal, would there be any point to life? And if a friend fails, because he is not a true friend, is one allowed to attack his character and his weaknesses? What is the value of a friendship in which one person loves the other for his virtue, his loyalty, his steadfastness? What is the value of a love that expects loyalty? Isn't it our duty to accept the faithless friend as we do the faithful one who sacrifices himself? Is disinterest not the essence of every human relationship? That the more we give, the less we expect? And if a man gives someone his trust through all the years of his youth and stands ready to make sacrifices for him in manhood because of that blind, unconditional devotion, which is the highest thing any one person can offer another, only then to witness the faithlessness and base behavior of his friend, is he permitted to rise up in protest and demand vengeance? And if he does rise up and demand vengeance, having been deceived and abandoned, what does that say about the validity of his friendship in the first place? You see, these are the kinds of theoretical questions that have occupied me since I have been alone. Of course, solitude did not provide me with any answers. Nor, in any complete sense, did books,

129

neither the ancient texts of Chinese, Jewish, and classical thinkers, nor contemporary tracts that spell everything out, absolutely bluntly, while all they're giving you is words and more words and not any articulation of the truth. Is there, in fact, anyone who has ever given words to the truth, and set them on paper? I thought about this a great deal after I began my reading and self-questioning. Time went by and life around me seemed somehow to darken, and the books and my memories started to mass together and pile up. And for every crumb of truth in any individual book, my memories provided a corresponding retort that human beings may learn everything they want about the true nature of relationships, but this knowledge will make them not one whit the wiser. And that is why we have no right to demand unconditional honor and loyalty from a friend, even when events have shown us that this friend was faithless."

"Are you quite certain," asks the guest, "that this friend was faithless?"

There is a long moment of silence. In the deep shadows of the room and the uneasy flickering of the candlelight, they seem small: two wizened old men looking at each other, almost invisible in the darkness.

"I am not quite certain," says the General. "That is also why you're here. It's what we are discussing." He leans back in his chair and crosses his arms calmly and with military precision. He says, "There is such a thing as factual truth. This and this happened. These things happened in this and this fashion and at this and this time. It isn't hard to establish these things. The facts speak for themselves, as the saying goes; in the last years of our lives, facts confess themselves in ways that scream more loudly than a victim being tortured on the rack. By the end, everything has happened and the sum total is clear. And yet, sometimes facts are no more than pitiful consequences, because guilt does not reside in our acts but in the intentions that give rise to our acts. Everything turns on our intentions. The great, ancient systems of religious law I have studied all know and preach this. A man may commit a disloyal or base act, even the worst, even murder, and yet remain blameless. The act does not constitute the whole truth, it is always and only a consequence, and if one day any of us has to become a judge and pronounce sentence, it is not enough for us to content ourselves with the facts in the police report, we also have to acquaint ourselves with motive. The fact of your flight is easy to establish. But not your motive. Believe me, I have spent the last forty-one years turning over every possible reason for your incomprehensible act. No single examination of it led me to an answer. Only the truth can do that now."

"You said 'flight,'" says Konrad. "That's a strong word. In the final analysis, I owed nobody an accounting—I had resigned my commission in the proper fashion, I left behind no messy debts, I had made no promise to anyone which I failed to fulfill. Flight, that's a strong word." His voice is grave as he straightens a little in his chair, but it also betrays a tremor that seems to suggest that the force of this declaration is not entirely sincere.

"Perhaps the word is too strong." The General nods. "But when you look at what happened from a certain distance, you must admit that it's not easy to find a less harsh one. You say you didn't owe anyone anything. That is, and is not, true. Of course you didn't owe anything to your tailor or to the moneylenders in town. Nor did you owe me money or the fulfillment of any promise. And still, that July—you see, I remember everything, even the day, it was a Wednesday—when you left town, you knew that you were leaving behind a debt. That evening, I went to your apartment, because I had heard that you had gone away. I heard it at dusk, under peculiar circumstances. We can talk about those, too, sometime, if you would care to. I went to your apartment, where the only person to receive me was your manservant. I asked him to leave me alone in the room where you lived those last years when you were serving in the city." He falls silent, leans back and puts a hand over his eyes, as if looking back into the past. Then, calmly, in an even tone, he continues. "Of course, the manservant did as asked—what else could he do? I was alone in the room where you had lived. I took a good look at everything—you must excuse this tactless curiosity, but somehow I was incapable of accepting the fact, just could not believe that the person with whom I had spent the greater and the best part of my life, twenty-four years from childhood through youth and into adulthood, had simply bolted. I tried to justify it. I thought: Maybe he's seriously ill. Then I hoped perhaps you had temporarily lost your mind, or maybe someone had come after you because you had lost at cards or done something against the regiment, or the flag, or you'd broken your word or betrayed your honor. That sort of thing. You should not be surprised that any of these things struck me as less of a transgression than what you had actually done. Any of them would have had some justification, some explanation, even the betrayal of the ideals that shaped our world. Only one thing was incomprehensible: that you had committed a sin against me. You ran away like a swindler or a thief, you ran a matter of hours after leaving the castle where you had been with Krisztina and me, the three of us spending our days together, sometimes long into the night, as we had done for years, in mutual friendship and the brotherly trust that only twins can share, because they are sports of nature, bound together in life and death, aware, even when they are grown up and separated by great distances, of everything about each other. It doesn't matter if one lives in London and the other in a foreign country, both will fall ill at the same moment, and of the same

138

disease. They don't talk to each other, they don't write, they live in different circumstances, they eat different foods, they are thousands of miles apart, and yet when they are thirty or forty years old they suffer the same affliction, be it in the gallbladder or the appendix, and their chances of survival will be the same. Their two bodies are as organically linked as they were in the womb. And they love or hate the same people. It is a phenomenon of nature, not that common, but then again, not as rare as is usually thought.

"And sometimes, I've thought that friendship is formed of links as fateful as those between twins.

"A strange identity of impulses, sympathies, tasks, temperaments, and cultural formation binds two people together in a single fate. It does not matter what one of them may do against the other, that fate will remain the same. One of them may flee the other, but each will still know the other's essence. One of them may find a new friend or a new lover, but without the other's tacit consent this doesn't release their bond. Their lives will unfold along similar paths whether one of them goes far away or not, even as far as the tropics. These were some of the things I was thinking as I stood in your room the day you ran away.

"I still see that moment with absolute clarity. I still smell that smell of heavy English tobacco, I still see the furniture, the divan with the big oriental rug, and the equestrian pictures on the walls. And a dark red leather armchair, the kind you usually find in smoking rooms. The divan was very large, and you had obviously had it made to your own specifications, because there was nothing resembling it to be bought in the area. In fact, it wasn't a divan, more a French bed, large enough for two people."

He watches the smoke from his cigar.

"The window overlooked the garden, if I remember correctly. . . . It was the first and last time I was ever there; you never wanted me to visit you. And it was only by chance that you mentioned that you had rented a house on the outskirts of town in a deserted neighborhood, a house with a garden. That was three years before you fled—forgive me, I see that the word disturbs you."

"Please continue," says the guest. "Words are not the issue here."

"Do you think so?" asks the General innocently.

"Are words not the issue? I would not be bold enough to assert such a thing. Sometimes it seems to me that it is precisely the words one utters, or stifles, or writes, that are the issue, if not the only issue. Yes, I am sure," he continues firmly, "you had not ever invited me to this apartment, and without an invitation, I could not visit you. If I'm honest, I thought you were ashamed of letting me see this apartment you had furnished yourself, because I was a rich man. . . . Perhaps it seemed wanting. . . . You were a very proud man," he says, in the same firm voice. "The only thing that came between us when we were young was money. You were proud, and could not forgive that I am rich. Later in life I came to think that perhaps wealth is indeed unforgivable. To find oneself constantly the guest of a financial fortune . . . and on such a scale. I was born into it, and even I had the feeling from time to time that it was impermissible. And you were always painfully intent on underlining the financial imbalance between us. The poor, particularly the poor among the upper classes of society, do not forgive," he says with a strange tone of satisfaction. "And that is why I thought that perhaps you were hiding the apartment from me, perhaps you were ashamed of its simple furnishings. A foolish supposition, as I now know, but your pride was truly boundless. And so one day I find myself standing in the home that you had rented and furnished and never shown to me. And I do not believe my eyes. This apartment, as you well know, was a work of art. Nothing large, one generous room on the ground floor, two small ones upstairs, and yet everything—furniture, rooms, garden—arranged as only an artist could. That was when I understood that you really are an artist. And I also understood to what extent you were a stranger among the rest of us ordinary people. And also what wrong was done to you when, out of love and pride, you were given to the military life. No, you were never a soldier—and I could feel, in retrospect, the profound loneliness you felt among us. But this home served you as a refuge, just as in the Middle Ages a fortress or a cloister sheltered those who had renounced the world. And like a brigand you used this place to hoard everything of beauty and noble quality: curtains and carpets, silver, ancient bronzes, crystal and furniture, rare woven materials. . . . I know that your mother died at some point during those years, and that you also must have received inheritances from your Polish relatives. Once you mentioned a piece of property on the border with Russia, and the fact that you would inherit it. And now here it was, in these three rooms, exchanged for furniture and pictures. And in the middle of the main room downstairs, a piano, with a piece of ancient brocade thrown across it, and set on top, a crystal vase holding three orchids. The only place they grow in this region is in my greenhouse. I walked through the rooms and took mental inventory of everything. I grasped that you had lived among us and yet never belonged with us. I grasped that you had created this masterpiece of a rare and hidden retreat in secret, defiantly, as a great act of will, in order to conceal it from the world, as a place where you could live only for yourself and your art. Because you are an artist, and perhaps you could have created true artworks," he says, in a tone that brooks no contradiction. "That is what I read in the perfect selection of the furnishings in your abandoned apartment. And in that moment, Krisztina stepped through the door." He crosses his arms again and speaks so dispassionately and deliberately that he might be dictating the details of an accident to a policeman.

"I was standing in front of the piano, looking at the orchids," he says. "The apartment was like a disguise. Or was, perhaps, our uniform your disguise? Only you can answer that question, and now . . . everything is over, you have in fact provided the answer in the life you chose. One's life, viewed as a whole, is always the answer to the most important questions. Along the way, does it matter what one says, what words and principles one chooses to justify oneself? At the very end, one's answers to the questions the world has posed with such relentlessness are to be found in the facts of one's life. Questions such as: Who are you? . . . What did you actually want? . . . What could you actually achieve? . . . At what points were you loyal or disloyal or brave or a coward? And one answers as best one can, honestly or dishonestly; that's not so important. What's important is that finally one answers with one's life. You set aside your uniform because you saw it as a disguise, that much is already clear. I, on the other hand, wore mine for as long as duty and the world demanded it; that was my answer. So that settles one question. The other one is: What were you to me? Were you my friend? Because you fled without saying farewell—although not entirely, because the previous day something happened during the hunt, and it was only later that its meaning dawned on me: that it had been your farewell. One rarely knows when a word or an act will trigger some final, irreversible alteration in any relationship. Why did I go to your apartment that day? You did not ask me to come, you did not say your farewells, you left no word behind you. What was I doing—there in a place to which I had never been invited, on the very same day that you left us? What presentiment made me take the carriage and drive into town as fast as I could, to look for you in your apartment, which was already empty of life? . . . What was it that I had learned the previous day during the hunt? Has some piece of information been left out? . . . Did I have no confidential tip, no hint, no word that you were preparing to flee? . . . No, everyone was silent, even Nini. . . . You remember my old nurse, she knew everything there was to know about us. Is she still alive? Yes, in her own fashion. She lives like that tree there outside the window, the one planted by my great-grandfather. Like all of us, she has her allotted span of years, and hers is not yet complete. Nini knew. But not even she said anything.

"During those days, I was quite alone. And yet I knew that it was the moment when the time had come for everything to become clear and fall into place, you, me, everybody. Yes, that's what I understood out on the hunt," he says, lost in his memories and also answering a question he must often have asked himself.

"What did you understand?" asked Konrad.

"It was a beautiful hunt," says the General, his voice almost warm, as if he is reliving the particulars of a favorite memory. "The last big hunt in this forest. There were huntsmen then, real huntsmen . . . perhaps they still exist today, I don't know. That was the last time I went hunting in my forest. Since that time the only people who come are Sunday hunters, guests, who are received and taken care of by the steward and play around with their guns among the trees. The real hunt was something else entirely. You won't be able to understand that, because you were never a huntsman. It was just another duty, one of those professional duties appropriate to your rank, like riding and attending social gatherings. You were a huntsman, but only in the way of someone bowing to social customs.

"When you were out hunting, there would be a scornful look on your face, and you always carried your gun carelessly, as if it were a walking stick. You are a stranger to this oddest of passions, the most secret of all in a man's life, that burns deep inside him like magma, deeper than any role he plays, or clothes he wears, or refinements he learns. It's the passion for killing. We are human beings, and it is part of our human condition to kill. It's an imperative . . . we kill to protect, we kill to keep hold, we kill in revenge. You're smiling in scorn. . . . You were an artist, and these base, raw instincts had been refined out of your artist's soul? Maybe you think you never killed a living creature. But that is by no means certain." His voice is stern and precise. "This is the evening when there is no point in discussing anything but the essentials and the truth, because there will be no second such meeting, and maybe there are not many evenings and days left to either of us. . . . I am sure there will never be another one with greater significance. Perhaps you remember I, too, was once in the Orient a long time ago; it was on my honeymoon with Krisztina. We traveled all through the Arabian lands, and in Baghdad we were the guests of an Arabian family. They are the most distinguished people, as you, after all your travels, certainly know for yourself. Their pride, their hauteur, their bearing, their fiery natures and their calm, their disciplined bodies and confident movements, their games, the flash in their eyes, all demonstrate a primeval sense of rank, not social rank but man's first awakening in the chaos of creation to an understanding of his human dignity.

"There is a theory that at the beginning of time, long before the formation of peoples and tribes and cultures, the human species came into being there, deep in the Arabian world. Perhaps that explains their pride, I don't know. I'm not well-versed in these matters . . . but I do understand something about pride. And in the way one can sense, without any external evidence, that someone is of the same race and social rank, I sensed during those weeks in the Orient that the people there have a grandeur, including even the dirtiest camel driver. As I said, we were living with a local family, in a house that was like a palace; our ambassador had been kind enough to arrange the invitation. Those cool, white houses . . . do you know them? Each with its central courtyard, where the whole life of the family and the clan is conducted, so it is like a weekly market, a parliament, and a temple forecourt all rolled into one . . . the way they saunter, their eagerness to play that shows in all their movements. And that dignified, determined idleness, behind which their exuberance and passions lurk like snakes behind stones in the hot sun.

"One evening our hosts invited Arab guests in our honor. Until then, their hospitality had been more or less in the European style; the owner of the house was both a judge and a dealer in contraband, one of the wealthiest men in the city. The guest rooms had English furniture, the bathtub was made of solid silver. But on this particular evening we saw something quite other. The guests arrived after sundown, only men, grand gentlemen with their servants. In the middle of the courtyard the fire was already lit, burning with that acrid smoke that comes from camel dung. Everyone sat down around it in silence. Krisztina was the only woman present.

A lamb was brought, a white lamb, and our host took his knife and killed it with a movement I shall never forget . . . a movement like that is not something one learns, it is an Oriental movement straight out of the time when the act of killing still had a symbolic and religious significance, when it denoted sacrifice. That was how Abraham lifted the knife over Isaac when he was preparing to sacrifice him, that was the movement in the ancient temples when the sacrifice was made at the altar before the idols or the image of the godhead, and that was the movement that struck John the Baptist's head from his body . . . it is utterly ancient. In the Orient it is innate to every man. Perhaps it is what first distinguished humans as a species, after the interval when they were part human, part animal. . . .

"According to current wisdom, being human began with the opposable thumb, which made it possible to pick up a weapon or a tool. But perhaps being human begins with the soul and not the thumb. I don't know. . . . The Arab slaughtered the lamb, and as he did so, this old man in his white burnous, which remained unspotted by blood, was like an oriental high priest performing the sacrifice.

His eyes gleamed, for a moment he was young again, and all around him there was absolute silence. They sat around the fire, they watched the act of killing, the flash of the knife, the twitching of the lamb, the jet of blood, and their eyes gleamed also. And then I realized that these people are still intimately familiar with the act of killing, blood is something they know well, and the flash of the knife is as natural to them as the smile of a woman, or the rain. We understood—and I think Krisztina did, too, because at that moment she was seized with emotion, she blushed, then went white, breathed with difficulty, and turned her head away, as if she were witness to some passionate encounter—we understood that people in the East still retain their knowledge of the sacred symbolism of killing and its inner spiritual meaning. These dark, noble faces were all smiling, they pursed their lips and grinned in a kind of ecstasy as they watched, as if the killing were a warm, happy event, like an embrace. Curious, that in Hungarian our words for killing and embracing echo and heighten each other.*

*Ölés and ölelés

"Well, of course we are westerners," he says in another voice, sounding suddenly professional. "Westerners, or at least immigrants who settled here. For us, killing is a question of law and morality, or medicine, at any rate a sanctioned or prohibited act that is very precisely delineated within our system of thought. We kill, too, but in a more complicated way; we kill according to the dictates and authorization of the law. We kill to protect high principles and important human values, we kill to preserve the social order. It cannot be any other way. We are Christians, we have a sense of guilt, we are the product of Western civilization. Our history, right up to the present, is filled with mass murder, but whenever we speak of killing, it is with eyes lowered and in tones of pious horror; we cannot do otherwise, it is our prescribed role. There is only the hunt," he says, suddenly sounding almost happy. "Even then, we observe rules that are both chivalrous and practical, we protect the game according to the demands of the situation in any particular area, but the hunt is still a sacrifice, a distorted residue of what can still be recognized as a ritual that once formed part of a most ancient religious act. It is not true that the huntsman kills for the prize. That has never been the case, not even in prehistoric times, when hunting was one of the few ways to obtain food. The hunt was always surrounded by religious tribal ritual. The good huntsman was always the leader of his tribe and also in some fashion a priest. Over the course of time, all that has naturally faded, but even in their faded form, the rituals are still with us. In my whole life I think I have loved nothing so much as the first light of dawn on the day of a hunt. You get up in darkness, you put on clothes quite different from those you wear every day, and clothes that have been selected for a purpose, in a lamplit room you eat a breakfast that is quite different from the usual break-fast: you fortify your heart with schnapps and eat a slice of cold meat with it. I loved the smell of hunt-ing clothes; the felt was impregnated with scents of the forest, the leaves, the air and blood, because you had hung the birds you had shot from your belt, and their blood had dirtied the jacket. But is blood dirty? . . . I don't believe so. It is the most noble substance in the world, and in all eras the man who wished to say something inexpressibly grand to his God made a blood sacrifice. And the oily, metallic smell of the gun. And the raw, sour smell of the leather. I loved all of it," he says, sounding suddenly like an old man and almost ashamed, as if admitting to a weakness. "And then you step out of the house, your hunting comrades are already waiting, the sun isn't up yet, the gamekeeper is holding the dogs on the lead and gives a murmured report on the events of the previous night. You take your place in the shooting brake, and it starts to move. The countryside is beginning to stir, the forest stretches and rubs its eyes sleepily. Everything smells so clean, as if you have entered another homeland that existed once before, at the beginning of the world. The brake comes to a halt at the edge of the forest, you get out, your dog and your gamekeeper follow you silently. The wet leaves under the soles of your boots make almost no noise. The clearings are full of animal tracks. Now everything is coming to life around you. The light lifts and opens the roof of sky over the forest, as if the secret mechanism in the rigging-loft of a fairy-tale theater has begun to function. Now the birds are beginning to sing and a deer crosses the forest path a long way ahead, about three hundred paces in front of you. You pull back into the undergrowth, and watch. . . . The animal stands still: it cannot see you, it cannot smell you because the wind is in your face, and yet it knows that its fate is awaiting it somewhere close. It lifts its head, turns its delicate neck, its body tenses, for a few moments it stands motionless, rooted to the spot, the way one can be paralyzed by the inevitable, absolutely helpless, because one knows that the menace is no accidental piece of bad luck but the necessary consequence of incalculable and incomprehensible circumstances. Now you are already regretting that you are not carrying a cartridge pouch. You, too, stand frozen to the spot in the undergrowth; you, too, are bound inextricably to the moment; you, the huntsman. And you feel the tremor in your hands that is as old as man himself, you prepare for the kill and feel the forbidden joy, the strongest of all passions, the urge, neither good nor evil, that is part of all living creatures: the urge to be stronger, more skilled than your opponent, to preserve your concentration, to make no mistakes. The leopard feels it as he tenses for the spring, the snake feels it as she rears to strike among the rocks, the falcon feels it in his plummeting dive, and a man feels it when he has his quarry in his sights. And *you* felt it, Konrad, perhaps for the first time in your life, when you shouldered your gun and took aim, intending to kill me."

He bends over the little table that stands between them in front of the fireplace. He pours himself a sweet liqueur in a tiny glass and tests the surface of the crimson, syrupy liquid with the tip of his tongue, then, satisfied, sets the glass back down on the table again.

14

"It was still dark," he says, when the other man makes no reply, puts up no defense, gives no sign with a movement of the eye or hand that he has heard the accusation. "It was the moment that separates night from day, the underworld from the world above. And perhaps other things separate themselves out, too. It is the last second, when the depths and heights, the dark and the light, of the world and of men still brush against each other, when sleepers waken with a start from troubling dreams, when the sick begin to groan because they sense that the nightly hell is nearing its end and now the more distinct pain will begin again. Light and the natural ordering that accompanies the day will separate and tease out the layers of desire, the secret longings, the twitches of excitement that had been tangled in the darkness of the night. Both huntsmen and their game love this moment. It is no longer dark, it is not yet light. The forest smells so raw and wild, as if every living thing—plants, animals, people—were slowly coming back to consciousness in the dormitory of the world, exhaling all their secrets and bad thoughts.

"The wind stirs, too, at this moment, gently, carefully, like the sigh of a sleeping man as he senses the return of the earthly reality into which he was born. The scent of wet leaves, of ferns, of crumbling tree trunks, of rotting pine cones, of the soft carpet of fallen leaves and pine needles slippery from the dew, rises up from the earth to assault you like the smell of two lovers locked in sweat-soaked embrace. A magical moment, which our heathen ancestors used to celebrate deep in the forest, worshipfully, arms outstretched, facing East: earthbound man in the eternally recurring, spellbound expectation of light, insight, reason. This is the time when the game begins to move, heading for water. Night has still not quite ended, things are still happening in the forest, the nocturnal animals are still hunting, still ready, the wildcat is still on the watch, the bear is tearing the last scraps of flesh off his prey, the rutting stag still recalls the fury of the moonlit night and stands in the clearing where the sexual battle took place, raises his wounded head proudly, and surveys the scene with grave, bloodshot eyes, as if to fix the passion of that duel in his memory forever. In the heart of the forest night lives on, as does everything associated with it: prey, animal passion, the freedom to roam, pure love of life and the struggle for survival. It's the moment when something happens not just deep among the trees but also in the dark interior of the human heart, for the heart, too, has its night and its wild surges, as strong an instinct for the hunt as a wolf or a stag. The human night is filled with the crouching forms of dreams, desires, vanities, self-interest, mad love, envy, and the thirst for revenge, as the desert night conceals the puma, the hawk and the jackal. It is the moment when it is neither night nor day in man's heart, because the wild beasts have slunk out of the hidden corners of our souls, and something rouses itself, transmits itself from mind to hand, something we thought we had tamed and trained to obedience over the course of years, decades even. In vain, we have lied to ourselves about the significance of this feeling, but it has proved stronger than all our intentions, indissolvable, unrelenting. Every human relationship has a tangible core, and we can think about it, analyze it all we want, it is unchangeable. The truth is that for twenty-four years you have hated me with a burning passion akin to the fire of a great affair—even love.

"You have hated me, and when any one emotion or passion occupies us entirely, the need for revenge crackles and glimmers among the flames that torment us. Passion has no footing in reason. Passion is indifferent to reciprocal emotion, it needs to express itself to the full, live itself to the very end, no matter if all it receives in return is kind feelings, courtesy, friendship, or mere patience. Every great passion is hopeless, if not it would be no passion at all but some cleverly calculated arrangement, an exchange of lukewarm interests. You have hated me, and that makes for as strong a bond as if you had loved me. Why did you hate me? . . . I have had plenty of time to think about it. You have never accepted either money from me or presents, you never allowed our friendship to develop into a real relationship of brothers, and if I had not been so young back then, I would have known that this was a danger signal. Whoever refuses to accept a part wants the whole, wants everything. You hated me as a child, from the very first moment we met at the academy, where the best our Empire had to offer were reared and educated; you hated me, because there was something in me that you lacked. What was it? What talent or quality? . . . You were always the better student, you were always unintentionally a chef d'oeuvre of diligence, goodness, and talent, for you possessed an instrument, in the true sense of that word, you had a secret—music. You were related to Chopin, you were proud and reserved.

"But deep inside you was a frantic longing to be something or someone other than you are. It is the greatest scourge a man can suffer, and the most painful. Life becomes bearable only when one has come to terms with who one is, both in one's own eyes and in the eyes of the world. We all of us must come to terms with what and who we are, and recognize that this wisdom is not going to earn us any praise, that life is not going to pin a medal on us for recognizing and enduring our own vanity or egoism or baldness or our potbelly. No, the secret is that there's no reward and we have to endure our characters and our natures as best we can, because no amount of experience or insight is going to rectify our deficiencies, our self-regard, or our cupidity. We have to learn that our desires do not find any real echo in the world. We have to accept that the people we love do not love us, or not in the way we hope. We have to accept betrayal and disloyalty, and, hardest of all, that someone is finer than we are in character or intelligence.

"Over the course of my seventy-five years here in the middle of the forest, I have learned this much. But you have not been able to accept it," he says softly, definitively. Then he stops, and his eyes stare blindly into the half-darkness.

After a pause, as if to excuse his guest, he starts again: "Of course, you didn't know any of this when you were a child. That was a magical time. With age, memory enlarges every detail and presents it in the sharpest outline. We were children and we were friends: that is a great gift and we should thank fate for it. But then your character took shape and you found it intolerable that something inside you was lacking, something that I had, whether it was in the genes, or came from my upbringing, or maybe the good Lord God . . . so what was this something? Was it some talent? Or was it just that people were indifferent to you, or occasionally hostile, whereas they smiled at me and gave me their trust? You despised this trust and these friendships, but at the same time you envied them desperately. You must have sensed—not in so many words, of course, but in some inchoate way—that anyone who is a general favorite is in some fashion a whore.

"There are people who are loved by everyone, who are always being spoiled and forgiven with a smile, and who are indeed too willing to please, a little whorish.

"You see, I'm no longer afraid of words," he says and smiles, as if to encourage similar candor in his guest. "Solitude brings knowledge, and then there is nothing to fear anymore. Those who have, in fact, been singled out as the favorites of the gods really do consider themselves to be the elect, and they present themselves to the world with overweening assurance. But if that is how you saw me, then you were mistaken, and your envy distorted your vision. I do not wish to defend myself, because what I want is the truth, and whoever does that must start the search inside himself. What you took to be God-given favor in me and around me was nothing more than instinctive trust. I believed the best of the world until the day . . . well, the day I stood in the room you had abandoned. Maybe it was that very trustingness that made people wish me well, trust me in turn, and offer me their friendship. There was something in me then—I am speaking of the past and of something so far away that I might as well be discussing a stranger or someone long dead—some kind of lightness and lack of preconceptions that disarmed people. There was a period of my life, ten years of my youth, when the world was tolerant of my presence and my needs. A time of grace. Everyone comes rushing toward you as if you are a conqueror to be fêted with wine and wreaths of flowers and girls. And indeed throughout that decade in Vienna, in the academy and then the regiment, I never once lost the certainty that the gods had set a secret invisible ring on my finger that would always bring me luck and protect me from severe disappointments, and that I was surrounded by trust and affection. No one could ask more of life, it is the greatest blessing of all." He pauses, and his tone darkens.

"But if anyone allows it to go to his head, or becomes presumptuous or arrogant, or loses the humility to remember that fate is indulging him, or fails to understand that this golden situation can last only as long as we refrain from turning the gold into cheap coin and squandering it, he will go under. The world spares only those who remain modest and humble—and even then only for an interval, no more. You hated me," he says flatly. "As youth slowly passed, as the magic childhood faded, our relationship began to cool. There is no feeling sadder or more hopeless than the cooling of a friendship between two men. Between a man and a woman a delicate web of terms and conditions is always negotiated. Between men, on the other hand, the deep sense of friendship rests on its selflessness: we expect no sacrifices, no tenderness from each other, all we want is to preserve a pact wordlessly made between us. Perhaps

I was really the guilty one, because I did not know you well enough. I accepted that you did not reveal yourself completely to me, I admired your intelligence and your strange, bitter pride, I wanted to believe that you would forgive me as other people did because of this happy capacity I had to circulate in the world and to be welcomed, while you were only tolerated—I hoped for your forbearance of the fact that I was on easy terms with others, and I thought you might be pleased on my behalf. Ours was a friendship out of the ancient sagas. And while I walked in the sunshine of life, you chose to remain in the shadows. Is that also how you see it?"

"You were speaking of the hunt," says Konrad evasively.

"Yes, I was," says the General. "But all this is part of it. When one man decides to kill another, much has happened already; he does not simply load his gun and take aim. For example, what happens may be what I have been talking about, namely that you couldn't forgive me. What happened was that once upon a time two children had a friendship that bound them so delicately together, that they might have been living cradled in the huge dreaming pads of a great water lily—do you remember how for years I grew those rare-flowering 'Victoria Reginas' here in the greenhouse?—and then one day suddenly their bond cracked and broke. The magical time of childhood was over, and two grown men stood there in their place, enmeshed in a complicated and enigmatic relationship commonly covered by the word 'friendship.' We have to acknowledge this before we can talk about the hunt. One is not most guilty in the moment when one aims a weapon to kill someone. The guilt already exists, the guilt is in the intention. And if I say that this bond broke one day, then I have to know whether that is really true or not, and if it is, then I have to know who or what broke it. We were quite different, but we belonged together, we were more than the sum of our two selves, we were allies, we made our own community, and that is rare in life. Whatever fundamental thing was lacking in you was counterbalanced by the overabundance the world gave me. We were friends." He says this very loudly. "Understand, if you don't know it already. But you must have known it, both early on and then later, in the tropics or wherever else. We were friends, and the word carries a meaning only men understand. It is time you learned its full implication. We weren't comrades or companions or fellow-sufferers. Nothing in life can replace what we had. No all-consuming love could offer the pleasures that friendship brings to those it touches. If we had not been friends, you would not have raised your gun against me that morning on the hunt in the forest. And if we had not been friends, I would not have gone next day to the apartment to which you had never invited me, where you hoarded the dark incomprehensible secret that poisoned things between us. And if you were not my friend, you would not have fled the city that day, fled my presence and the scene of the crime like a murderer and a criminal; you would have stayed, you would have deceived and betrayed me, and that might well have hurt me deeply, wounded my vanity and my sense of self, but none of that would have been as terrible as what you did. Because you were my friend. And if that had not been true, you would not have come back after forty-one years, again like a murderer or a criminal stealing back to the scene of the crime.

"You had to come back; you know it. And now I have to say something that only very slowly became

168

clear to me and that I kept denying; I have to acknowledge a discovery that both surprises and disturbs me: we are still, even now, friends.

"Evidently there is no external power that can alter human relationships. You killed something inside me, you ruined my life, but we are still friends. And tonight, I am going to kill something inside you, and then I shall let you go back to London or to the tropics or to hell, and yet still you will be my friend. This too is something we both need to know before we talk about the hunt and everything that happened afterwards. Friendship is no ideal state of mind; it is a law, and a strict one, on which the entire legal systems of great cultures were built. It reaches beyond personal desires and self-regard in men's hearts, its grip is greater than that of sexual desire, and it is proof against disappointment, because it asks for nothing. One can kill a friend, but death itself cannot undo a friendship that reaches back to childhood; its memory lives on like some act of silent heroism, and indeed there is in friendship an element of ancient heroic feats, not the clash of swords and the rattle of sabers, but the selfless human act. And as you raised the gun to kill me, our friendship was more alive than ever before in the twenty-four years we had known each other. One remembers such moments because they become part of the content and meaning of the rest of one's life. And I remember. We were standing in the undergrowth between the pines. The clearing opens away from the path there and continues into the dense woodland where the forest is still virgin and dark. I was walking ahead of you and stopped because far ahead, about three hundred paces away, a deer had stepped out from between the trees.

"It was gradually getting light, slowly, as if the sun were stalking the world, feeling it very gently with the tips of its rays. The animal stood still at the edge of the clearing and looked into the undergrowth, sensing danger. Instinct, the sixth sense that is more acute than smell or sight, moved in the nerves of its body. It could not see us and it was upwind from us, so the morning breeze could not warn it; we stood motionless for a long time, already feeling the strain of keeping absolutely still—I in front, between the trees at the edge of the clearing; you behind me. The gamekeeper and the dog were some distance back. We were alone in the forest in the solitude that is part night, part dawn, part trees, and part animals, that gives one the momentary sensation that one has lost one's way in the world and must someday retrace one's steps to this wild and dangerous place that is truly home. It's a feeling I always had when out hunting. I saw the animal and stopped. You saw it, too, and stopped ten paces behind me. That is the moment when both quarry and hunter are utterly alert, sensing the entirety of the situation and the danger, even if it's dark, even without turning the head. What forces or rays or waves transmit knowledge at such a time? I have no idea. . . . The air was clear. The pines were unruffled by the faint breeze. The animal listened. It did not move a muscle, stood as if spellbound, for every danger contains within it a spell, an enchantment. When fate turns to face us and calls our name, along with the oppression and the fear we feel is a kind of attraction, because we do not only want to live, no matter what the cost, we want to know our fate and accept it, even at the cost of danger and death. That is what the deer must have been experiencing just then.

"Just as I was, as I clearly remember. And you,

too, a few paces behind me—you were as mesmerized as the beast and I, both of us in front and in range of you as you lifted the safety catch with that quiet, cold click that is the sound of perfectly tempered steel going about its fatal task, whether it is a dagger crossing another or a fine English rifle being cocked for the kill. Do you remember?"

"Yes," says the guest.

"A classic moment," says the General with almost a connoisseur's pleasure. "I was the only one to hear the click, it was too quiet to carry three hundred paces to the deer, even through the silence of dawn.

"And then something happened that I could never prove in a court of law, but that I can tell you because you know it already—it was a little thing, I felt you move, more clearly than if I'd been watching you. You were close behind me, and a fraction to the side. I felt you raise your gun, set it to your shoulder, take aim, and close one eye. I felt the gun slowly swivel. My head and the deer's head were in the exact same line of fire, and at the exact same height; at most there may have been four inches between the two targets. I felt your hand tremble, and I knew as surely as only the hunter can assess a particular situation in the woods, that from where you were standing you could not be taking aim at the deer. Please understand me: it was the hunting aspect, not the human, that held my attention right then. I was, after all, a devotee of hunting, with some expertise in its technical problems, such as the angle at which one must position oneself in relation to a deer standing unsuspecting at a distance of three hundred paces. Given the geometrical arrangement of the marksman and the two targets, the whole thing was quite clear, and I could calculate what was going on in the mind of the person behind my back. You took aim for half a minute, and I knew that down to the second, without a watch. I knew you were not a fine shot and that all I had to do was move my head a fraction and the bullet would whistle past my ear and maybe hit the deer. I knew that one movement would suffice and the bullet would remain in the barrel of your gun. But I also knew I couldn't move because my fate was no longer mine to control: some moment had come, something was going to happen of its own volition. And I stood there, waiting for the shot, waiting for you to pull the trigger and put a bullet through the head of your friend. It was a perfect situation: no witnesses, the gamekeeper and the dogs were a long way back, it was one of those well-known 'tragic accidents' that are detailed every year in the newspapers. The half minute passed and still there was no shot. Suddenly the deer smelled danger and exploded into motion with a single bound that took him out of our sight to safety in the undergrowth. We still didn't move. And then, very slowly, you let the gun sink.

"I could not see or hear that movement, either, but I knew it as well as if I were facing you. You lowered the gun so carefully in case even the air moving over the barrel might make a whisper and betray you, now that the moment to take the shot was gone and the deer had vanished.

"You see, the interesting thing is that you still could have killed me, there were no witnesses, and no judge would have convicted you, everyone would have rushed to surround you with sympathy, because we were the legendary friends, Castor and Pollux, together for twenty-four years through thick and thin, we were their reincarnation. If you had killed me, everyone would have reached out to you, everyone would have mourned with you, because the world believes there could be no more tragic figure than someone who accidentally kills his friend. What man, what prosecutor, what lunatic would make the unbelievable accusation that you had done it deliberately? There is absolutely no proof that you were harboring any deadly animosity toward me. The previous evening, we had all dined together—my wife, my relations, our hunting comrades—as a friendly circle in the castle where you had been welcome, no matter what the day, for decades, everyone had seen us together just as we always were, in the regiment and in society, as warm and affectionate as ever. You did not owe me any money, you lived in my house like a member of the family, who could imagine you would do such a thing? No one. What cause would you have to murder me? Who could be inhuman enough to imagine that you, my friend-of-friends, would kill me, your friend-of-friends, when you could ask anything in life of me, receive anything you needed by way of psychological or material support, treat my house as yours, my fortune as yours to share, my family as your second family?

"Any accusation would have rebounded on

whoever made it; the world would have punished it as a piece of insolence, and then rushed to comfort you again.

"That is how things stood. And yet you didn't fire. Why? What happened in that moment? Was it just that the deer sensed the danger and fled, whereas human nature is constructed in such a way that when we have to accomplish some action that is utterly abnormal, we need some objective pretext? Your plan was the right one, it was both precise and perfect, but perhaps it required the presence of the deer; the scene had come apart, and you let your gun drop. It was a matter of fractions of a second; who could divide everything up into its constituent parts, see them separately and make a judgment? And it's really not important. The fact is what matters, even if it would not determine a trial. You wanted to kill me, and when something unanticipated disrupted the moment, your hand began to tremble and you didn't do it. The deer was already out of sight between the trees, we didn't move, I didn't turn around. We stood like that for some seconds. If I had looked you in the face just then, I might have seen it all. But I didn't dare. There's a feeling of shame that is more painful than any other in life; it's the shame felt by the victim who is forced to look his killer in the eyes, as if he were the creature bowing before its creator. That's why I didn't look at you, and as the paralysis left us, I started to walk across the clearing toward the top of the hill. You started mechanically to move behind me. As we went, without turning around, I said, 'You missed your shot.'

"You didn't say a word, and your silence was its own admission. At times like that, anyone would start talking, either ashamed or worked up, trying to explain himself, making jokes or sounding insulted: every huntsman wants to prove that he was right, that the animal was a poor specimen, that the distance was too great, that the shot was too risky . . . but you said nothing. And your silence meant, 'Yes, I missed the shot that should have killed you.' We reached the top of the hill without a word being exchanged. The gamekeeper was already up there with the dogs, the valley was echoing with shots, the hunt had begun. Our paths separated. When midday came and it was time to eat—a table and food for the huntsmen had been set up under the trees—your beater told me you had left for town."

The guest picks up another cigar. His hands betray no tremor, he calmly cuts the tip. The General leans forward, holding a candle, to light it for him.

"Thank you," says the guest.

"But that evening, you came to dinner," says the General. "As you always did, every evening. You came at the usual time, seven-thirty, in the carriage. And as on so many evenings we dined à trois with Krisztina.

"The table was laid in the great dining room, as it was tonight, and with the same ornamental figures, and Krisztina sat between us. There were blue candles burning. She liked candlelight, she liked everything that echoed tradition, and times past, and a nobler form of human discourse. After the hunt was over, I had gone directly to my rooms to change, and had not seen Krisztina that afternoon. The manservant had told me that she had left after luncheon for town. As I came into the room, Krisztina was sitting in front of the fireplace with a light Indian shawl around her shoulders, for the weather was misty and damp. A fire had been lit; she was reading and did not hear me. Perhaps the rugs absorbed the sound of my footsteps, perhaps she was simply too absorbed in the text—it was an English book, a traveler's description of the tropics—but in any case she did not become aware of me until I was standing right in front of her. Then she looked up—do you remember her eyes? She had a way of looking up that turned the world to brilliant daylight—and maybe it was the effect of the candlelight, but I was shocked by her pallor. 'Are you feeling unwell?' I asked her. She said nothing. She stared at me for a long moment, wide-eyed, and those seconds were almost as drawn out and as eloquent as the moments that morning in the forest when I stood still, waiting to see whether you would say something or squeeze the trigger. She scrutinized my face as if her life depended on finding out what I was thinking if I was thinking . . . if there was something I knew. . . . At that moment, knowledge was more important than life itself. The thing that is always the most important—more important than the outcome, more important than the prey—is to know what the creature we have chosen as our victim thinks of us. . . . She looked into my eyes as if she were conducting an interrogation. I believe I returned her gaze steadily. During those seconds, and later, I was calm, and my face betrayed nothing to her. Indeed, during that morning and afternoon, on that strange hunt in which I had become the game, I had struggled to reach the decision that, no matter what life brought, I would remain silent and I would never, ever, speak either to Krisztina or to Nini, the two people who were my confidantes, of what I had been forced to realize in the dawn out in the woods. I had also decided to have a doctor observe you as unobtrusively as possible, since some demon of insanity seemed to have taken hold of your brain. I could think of no other explanation. The man closest to my heart has gone mad, is what I kept repeating to myself, constantly, obstinately, despairingly, all morning, all afternoon, and that is how I saw you when you came in. I was trying to preserve human dignity in general and yours in particular, for if you were the master of your faculties and had a reason—no matter what it was—to take up a weapon against me, then every one of us who lived in this house had lost our human dignity, including Krisztina and myself. That is also how I interpreted the look of shock and astonishment in Krisztina's eyes when I stood before her after the hunt. That she intuited the secret that had bound you and me since the morning.

"Women sense these things, I thought. Then you come, in evening dress, and we go in to table. We chat as we did on other evenings. We talk about the hunt, about the beaters' report, about the error made by one of the huntsmen who had shot a buck he had no right to shoot . . . but we do not say a single word all evening about those strange, questionable seconds. You do not mention your own hunting adventure with the magnificent deer you failed to kill. Such a story requires a telling, even when one is less than an expert huntsman. You don't say a word about missing the game and leaving the hunt early without explanation and going back to town, not to reappear until evening, although it is all very irregular and a breach of etiquette. You could mention the morning in a single word . . . but you don't. It's as if we had not gone on the hunt at all. You talk about other things. You ask Krisztina what she was reading as you came into the salon to join us. You and she have a long discussion about it, you ask Krisztina what the title is, you want to know what impression she has of the text, you have her tell you what life in the tropics is like, you behave as if this subject matter is of burning interest to you—and it is not until later that I learn from the bookseller in town that this book and others on the same subject were ordered by you, and that you had lent it to Krisztina a few days before. I know none of that yet. You both cut me out of the conversation, because I know nothing about the tropics. Later, when I realize that you had been deceiving me that night, I think back to this scene, I hear the words, even though they faded long ago, and I am forced to admit, in genuine admiration, that the two of you played your roles perfectly. I, the uninitiated, can find nothing suspicious in your words: you talk about the tropics, about a book, about an ordinary piece of reading. You want to know what Krisztina thinks, you are particularly interested in whether someone born and raised in another part of the world could tolerate the conditions in the tropics . . . what does she think? (You don't ask me.) And could she herself tolerate the rain, the warm haze, the suffocating hot mists, the loneliness in the swamps and the primeval forest . . . you see, the words come back of their own accord. The last time you sat in this armchair, forty-one years ago, you talked about the tropics, the swamps, the warm mists, and the rain. And just now, when you returned to this house, there they were again, words like swamp, and the tropics, and rain, and hot mist. Yes, words come back. Everything comes back, words and things go round in a circle, sometimes they circle the entire globe and then they finally return to their starting point and something is completed," he says calmly. "That was what you talked about, the last time you spoke to Krisztina. Around midnight, you order the carriage and are driven back to town. Those were the events on the day of the hunt," he says, and his voice expresses the satisfaction of an old man who has just successfully delivered an exact report, a systematic recapitulation that commands attention.

15

When you leave, Krisztina also withdraws," he says after a moment. "I remain alone in this room. She has left the English book on the tropics lying on her chair. I have no desire to go to sleep, so I pick up the book and thumb through it. I look at the pictures, and try to involve myself with its statistics about the economy and public health. It surprises me that Krisztina is reading such a book. All this won't concern her very much, I think, the mathematical curve of rubber production on the peninsula can't be that interesting to her, nor the general health problems of the natives. It's just not Krisztina, I think.

But the book has something to say, not just in English and not just about living conditions on the peninsula. As I am sitting there, book in hand, after midnight, alone in the room after the two people who have meant the most to me, aside from my father, have left, it suddenly dawns on me that the book is another signal. And I realize something else. During the day, things have finally begun to impose themselves on my attention, something has happened, life has turned eloquent. At such moments, I think, great care is required, because on such days life is speaking to us in mute signs, everything suddenly makes us alert, everything is a proof and a symbol, all we need to do is understand. One day things mature and we can put words to them. And, as I think this, I suddenly understand that this book is both a sign and an answer. It is saying: Krisztina wants to leave here. She is thinking about strange worlds, which means she must want something other than this world. Perhaps she wants to run away from here, from something or someone—and this someone can be me, but it can also be you. It is as clear as daylight, I think, Krisztina feels and knows something, and she wants to get away from here, and that's why she is reading a study of the tropics. I sense a great many things, and I feel that I also understand them. I feel and I understand what happened today: my life has split in two, like a landscape torn apart by an earthquake. On the one side is childhood, you and everything that the past has meant, and on the other is a dark place through which I cannot see, but through which I must find my way: the remainder of my life. And the two parts of this life are no longer in contact with each other. What happened? I cannot say. I have spent the whole day in an effort to appear calm and in control of myself, and I succeeded; Krisztina could not yet know anything as she looked at me, her face pale and with that strange questioning stare. She could not know, could not read on my face, what had happened on the hunt. . . . And indeed, what *had* happened? Am I not just imagining all this? Is the whole thing not just a figment of my imagination? If I tell it to anyone, he or she will probably laugh in my face. I have nothing, no proof, in my hand. . . . All I have is a voice inside me, stronger than any proof, crying out unmistakably, incontrovertibly, beyond all doubt, that I am not deceiving myself, and that I know the truth. And the truth is that in the dawn, my friend wanted to kill me. What a ridiculous accusation, out of the empty air, isn't it? Can I ever speak about this conviction, which is even more horrifying than the thing itself, to another human being? No. But now that I am in possession of this knowledge, with that calm certainty that accompanies our recognition of simple facts, how am I to imagine our future lives together? Can I look you in the eye, or should all three of us, Krisztina, you, and I, play the game and turn our friendship into pure theater while we all watch one another?

"Is it possible to live in such a way? As I said before, I think that perhaps you have gone mad. I think, perhaps it is the music. One cannot be a musician and a relative of Chopin and escape unpunished. But at the same time, I know that this hope is both cowardly and foolish: I have to look truth in the face, I must not imagine things, you are not mad, there is no relief, no way out. You have a reason to hate me and to want to kill me. I cannot grasp what that reason is. There is one simple, natural explanation, namely that you have been smitten with a sudden, wild passion for Krisztina, and this, too, could be a form of madness. But this assumption is so implausible—there has been no trace, no sign whatever in the life the three of us have led together—that I have to discard it. I know Krisztina, I know you, and I know myself—at least I think I do. Our entire lives, our first acquaintance with Krisztina, my marriage, our friendship, it's all so open, so clean, so transparent, the personalities and the circumstances are so unambiguous, that I would have to be insane to believe any such thing even for a second. Passions, no matter how perverse, cannot be concealed; a passion that compels the man possessed by it to pick up his weapon one day and turn it against his closest friend cannot be hidden from the world for months on end. Even I, the perpetually blind and deaf third party, would have had to pick up some sign of it—we virtually live together; no week goes by in which you do not dine with me three or four times; during the day I am in town, in the barracks, serving alongside you; we know everything about each other. And I know Krisztina's days and nights, her body and her soul, as well as I know my own. It's a crazy notion, that you and Krisztina . . . and I am almost relieved when I make myself examine this notion. It must be something else. What happened is deeper, more mysterious, less comprehensible. I have to talk to you. Should I have someone observe you? Like the jealous husband in a comedy? I am not a jealous husband. Suspicion has trouble taking hold in my nervous system, I am calm when I think about Krisztina, whom I found the way a collector finds the prize of his life, the rarest, most perfect object in his collection, the masterpiece, the goal and meaning of his existence. Krisztina does not lie, Krisztina is not unfaithful, I know all her thoughts, even the secret ones that are thought only in dreams. The diary bound in yellow velvet that I gave her in the first days of our marriage tells everything, because we had agreed that she would write about her feelings and thoughts for me and for herself—her longings, her emotions, all the by-products of the soul that one dares not speak aloud because one is ashamed or sees them as irrelevant. She would sketch these out in the diary, share with me in a few words what she thought and felt under the influence of a particular person or a situation. . . . That is how deeply we trust each other. And the secret diary is always in the drawer of a desk to which only the two of us have keys. This diary is the most confidential thing there can be between a man and a woman. If there is a secret in Krisztina's life, it would have shown itself already in her diary. However, I realize, for some time now we have forgotten this secret game . . . and I stand up and walk through the dark house to Krisztina's study and look for the yellow diary. The drawer is empty."

He closes his eyes and sits there like that for some time, his face expressionless like a blind man's. He seems to be searching for a word.

"It is already after midnight, the house is asleep. Krisztina is tired, I don't want to disturb her. She has probably taken the diary with her to her room, I think to myself," he says amicably. "I don't want to disturb her, I will ask her tomorrow whether she was telling me something with the diary, in our secret sign language. For you see, this confidential little book which we do not discuss—we are each a little ashamed in front of the other about this silent confidence we share—is like a declaration of love that repeats itself again and again. Such things are hard to discuss. It was Krisztina's idea, she asked me for it in Paris, on our honeymoon, she was the one who wanted to make the confession—and it was only later, much later, after she had died, that I understood that one only prepares oneself so consciously to confess, to hew to the utmost honesty, if one knows that one day there will actually be something that requires confession. For a long time, I did not understand this diary, I thought these secret written messages, this Morse Code of her life, were a little exaggerated, a woman's whim. She said she never wanted to have secrets from me nor from herself, which is why she wanted to write down everything that otherwise would be hard to talk about. As I said, later I understood that someone who flees into honesty like that fears something, fears that her life will fill with something that can no longer be shared, a genuine secret, indescribable, unutterable. Krisztina wants to give me everything, her body, her soul, her feelings, and her innermost thoughts. . . . We are on our honeymoon, Krisztina is in love, think where she comes from, and what it means to her that I offer her my name, this castle, the palace in Paris, the wide world, all things she could not even have dreamed of a few months before in her small-town surroundings and in the modest house where she spent her days alone with a silent, sick old man who lived only for his instrument, his notebooks, and his memories . . . and suddenly life gives her everything with open hands, marriage, a year-long honeymoon, Paris, London, Rome, then the East, months in oases, the sea. Of course, Krisztina believes she is in love. Later she reaches the understanding that she is not in love, nor had she been, even back then. She is merely grateful."

He links his fingers, rests his arms on his knees and leans forward. "She is grateful, very grateful, in her way, the way of a young woman on her honeymoon with her husband, a rich, distinguished young man." He tightens the grip of his fingers and stares at the pattern in the carpet, sunk in thought. "She is determined to show her gratitude, and that is why she has the idea of the diary. This extraordinary present. For from the very first moment, it is filled with surprising admissions. Krisztina is not courting me, and her confessions are sometimes disturbingly candid. She describes me just as she sees me, in a few words, but to the point. She describes what doesn't please her about me, the way I am far too open with everyone in the world. She feels I lack modesty, which, with her religious temperament, she believes to be the greatest virtue. No, it is quite true that in those years I am not modest. The world is mine, I have found the woman who in every word, every movement of her body, every leap of her mind calls forth a complete echo in me, I am rich, I have position, the future opens itself before me like a shining path, I am thirty years old, I love life, I love military service, I love my career. Now, in retrospect, this hearty self-satisfaction and sense of good fortune make my head spin. And like everyone whom the gods spoil without reason, I feel a kind of anxiety buried at the heart of my happiness. It is all too beautiful, too flawless, too complete. Such unbroken happiness always arouses fear. I would like to make a sacrifice to fate, I would be glad if, coming into some new harbor, I were to receive mail from home, informing me of some financial or other unpleasantness. For example, that the castle had burned to the ground or that an investment had gone sour or that my banker had bad news for me or some such thing. . . . One always wants to repay the gods with some of one's good fortune. For it is well known that the gods are jealous, and that if they give a mortal a year of happiness, they immediately enter this debt on the ledger and demand repayment at the end of life with crippling interest. But everything around me is in perfect order. Krisztina writes short entries in her diary that read as if they had been composed in a dream. Sometimes she writes no more than a line or even just one word. For example: 'You are beyond hope, because you are vain.' Then nothing for weeks. Or she writes that she has seen a man in Algiers who has followed her in an alley and spoken to her, and she had the feeling she could go away with him.

"Krisztina is a restless, scintillating spirit, I think. But I am happy and even these strange disquieting outbursts of honesty are unable to disturb that happiness. It does not occur to me that someone who is so compulsive about revealing everything to another person is perhaps this honest precisely because she wishes to avoid having to confess something that to her is even more important and fundamental. I do not think of such a thing on my honeymoon; nor later, when I read the diary. But then comes that day and that night, the day of the hunt, when I feel as if your gun had gone off and the bullet had whistled past my ear. And then the night, when you leave us, but not before discussing the tropics with Krisztina in some detail. And I remain alone with the memory of that day and that evening. And I do not find the diary in its usual place in the drawer of Krisztina's desk. I decide to find you in town next day and ask. . . . "

He falls silent, and shakes his head in the manner of old people exclaiming over some piece of childishness.

"Ask what? . . ." he says quietly and dismissively, as if to mock himself. "What can one ask people with words? And what is the value of an answer given in words instead of in the coin of one's entire life? . . . Not much," he says firmly. "There are very few people whose words correspond exactly to the reality of their lives. It may be the rarest thing there is. But I did not know that then. I am not thinking now about pitiful liars. I am thinking that people find truth and collect experiences in vain, for they cannot change their fundamental natures. And perhaps the only thing in life one can do is to take the givens of one's fundamental nature and tailor them to reality as cleverly and carefully as one can. That is the most we can accomplish. And it does not make us any the cleverer, or any the less vulnerable . . . so I want to talk to you, and I still do not know that everything I can ask you and everything you can answer will not change the facts. Nevertheless, one can get closer to reality and the facts by using words, questions and answers, and that is why I want to talk to you. I go to sleep, exhausted, and sleep deeply, as if I had completed some great physical effort, a long ride, a long walk. . . . Once I carried a bear down from the mountains on my back. I know that I was exceptionally strong during those years, and yet I am still astonished in retrospect at how I managed to carry this great weight across slopes and through gullies. Evidently one endures anything, provided one has a goal. Back then I went to sleep in the snow in a similar state of exhaustion after I had reached the valley with the bear; my gamekeepers found me half-frozen next to its dead body. That was how I slept that night. Deep and dreamlessly. . . . After I wake up, I order the carriage and drive into town to your apartment. I stand in the room and realize that you have gone away. It is only next day that we receive your letters at the regimental barracks telling us that you are resigning your commission and going abroad. At that moment, all I understand is the fact of your flight, because now it is certain that you wanted to kill me, that something has happened and is still happening whose true significance I do not yet grasp, and it is also certain that it all has to do with me personally, that it's all happening to me as well as to you. So I stand in that mysterious room filled with beautiful objects as the door opens and in walks Krisztina."

He says all this as if he were spinning a tale, sweetly, amicably, to entertain his friend, now finally returned home from a far country and a distant time, with the more interesting parts of an old story.

Konrad listens without moving. His cigar has gone out and he has set it on the rim of the glass ashtray, he sits, arms folded, quite still, his posture stiff and correct, the perfect officer conversing pleasantly with another of higher rank.

"She opens the door and stops on the threshold," says the General. "She is not wearing a hat, she has come from home and has harnessed the light trap herself. 'Has he gone?' she asks. Her voice is strangely hoarse. I nod, yes, he has gone. Krisztina stands in the door, straight and slender, perhaps she was never so beautiful as in that moment. She has the pallor of the wounded who have lost a great deal of blood; only her eyes were fever-bright, as they had been the evening before, when I came up to her while she was reading. 'He has fled,' she says, and does not wait for an answer; she says it to herself, it's a statement of fact. 'The coward,' she adds softly and calmly."

"She said that?" asks the guest, abandoning his statuelike stillness and clearing his throat.

"Yes," says the General. "That is all. Nor do I ask her anything. We stand silently in the room. Then Krisztina begins to look around, she takes in the furniture, the paintings, the art objects one by one. I watch her. She looks around the room as if saying goodbye. She looks at it as if she had seen it all already and now she wants to take leave of every object in it. As you know, one can look at things or a room in one of two ways: as if seeing them for the first time or seeing them for the last. Krisztina's eyes show none of the curiosity of discovery. They move calmly, assuredly, through this room the way one checks a room at home to be sure that everything is in its place. Her eyes are shining like an invalid's and yet are strangely veiled. She doesn't say a word, and she is in control of herself, but I feel that this woman has been thrown out of the safe course of her life and that she is about to lose herself and you and me. One look, one unexpected movement, and she will do or say something that can never be repaired. . . . She looks at the pictures, calmly, without curiosity, as if to impress on her memory things she has often seen before and now sees one last time. She looks at the wide French bed with a proud look and blinks, then shuts her eyes for a moment. Then she turns, as wordless as she was on arrival, and leaves the room. I remain. Through the open window I watch her walk through the garden between the standard roses which have just begun to flower. She seats herself in the little trap which is waiting for her behind the fence, picks up the reins, and departs. A moment later the carriage has disappeared around the bend in the street."

He stops talking and looks over at his guest.

"Am I not tiring you?" he asks politely.

"No," says Konrad hoarsely. "Absolutely not. Please go on."

"I am going into quite a lot of detail," he says as if to excuse himself. "But it's not possible any other way: only in the details can we understand the essential, as books and life have taught me. One needs to know every detail, since one can never be sure which of them is important, and which word shines out from behind things. But I don't have much more to say. You have fled, Krisztina has driven home in the trap. And I, what is there left for me to do at this moment, and for the rest of my life? . . . I look at the room and then after the vanished Krisztina. I know that your manservant is standing at attention out in the hall. I call his name, he comes in and salutes. 'At your orders,' he says.

" 'When did the Captain leave?'. . . 'With the early express.' That's the train to the capital. 'Did he take much luggage?' 'No, only a few civilian clothes.' 'Did he leave any orders or any message?' 'Yes, this apartment is to be given up. The furniture is to be sold. The lawyer is to take care of it. I am to return to the unit,' he says. Nothing more.

"We look at each other. And then comes the moment that is not easy to forget. The fellow—a twenty-year-old farm boy, I'm sure you remember his good-humored, intelligent face—abandons his military posture and his straight-ahead parade ground stare, and he's no longer the common soldier standing in front of his superior, he's a man who knows something in front of a man he pities. There is something so human and sympathetic in his glance that I turn white, then red . . . now—for the first and only time in my life—I lose control, too. I step up to him, seize the front of his jacket, and almost lift him off his feet. We are breathing into each other's faces and looking straight into each other's eyes. The boy's are full of horror and, again, sympathy. You know how, back then, it was better for me never to seize hold of people or things; if I didn't touch things carefully, they broke. . . . I know that, too, and I sense that both of us, the boy and I, are in danger. So I let him down again, set him back on the floor rather like a lead soldier; his boots land with a thump on the parquet and he stands stiffly at attention again as if on parade. I take out my handkerchief and wipe my brow. There is only one question, and this person could answer it immediately: Has the lady who just left been here at other times? If he does not answer, I will kill him.

But if he answers, perhaps I will also kill him, and perhaps not just him ... at such times one does not know one's friends anymore. But in the same moment I know that it is superfluous. I know that Krisztina has been here before, not just once but many times."

He leans back and lets his arms drop wearily.

"Now there is no further point in asking anything. A stranger cannot betray what one still needs to know. One would need to know why all this happened. And where the boundary lies between two people. The boundary of betrayal. That is what one would need to know. And also, where in all this my guilt lies? ..."

He asks this very quietly, and his voice is uncertain. It is evident from his words that this is the first time he has uttered them aloud, after he has carried them in his soul for forty-one years and until now has found no answer.

16

Things do not simply happen to one," he says, his voice firmer now as he looks up. Above their heads the candles burn with high, guttering, smoky flames; the hollows surrounding the wicks are quite black. Outside, beyond the windows, the landscape and the town are invisible in the darkness; not a single lantern is burning in the night. "One can also shape what happens to one. One shapes it, summons it, takes hold of the inevitable. It's the human condition. A man acts, even when he knows from the very onset that his act will be fatal. He and his fate are inseparable, they have a pact with each other that molds them both. It is not true that fate slips silently into our lives. It steps in through the door that we have opened, and we invite it to enter. No one is strong enough or cunning enough to avert by word or deed the misfortune that is rooted in the iron laws of his character and his life. Did I know about you and Krisztina? I mean from the start, the beginning of our story à trois? . . . It was you who introduced me to Krisztina. You knew her as a child, it was you who used to have scores copied by her father when he was an old man who could still use his crippled hands to write out music but could no longer hold a violin and bow and coax rich tones out of them, so that he had to abandon his career in the concert hall for a small-town conservatory, where he taught all the unmusical or at best marginally musical pupils, and picked up an additional pittance by correcting and improving the compositions of gifted amateur dabblers. . . . That was how you met him and his daughter, who was then seventeen. Her mother died in the southern Tyrol, where she had gone to a sanitarium near her birthplace to receive care for her heart condition.

"Later, at the end of our honeymoon, we went

to this spa town to find the sanitarium, because Krisztina wanted to see the room where her mother had died.

"We arrive in Arco one afternoon in an automobile, after driving along the shores of Lake Garda in a drift of the scents of flowers and orange trees. We stop in Riva and that afternoon we go over to Arco. The countryside is silver-gray, as if covered in olive groves. High above is a fortress, and hidden in the warm, misty air between the cliffs is the sanitarium. There are palm trees everywhere, and the light is so delicately hazy that it is like being in a greenhouse. In the stillness, the pale-yellow building where Krisztina's mother spent her last years looks mysterious, as if it were home to all the sadness that can afflict the human heart, and as if heart disease itself were the consequence of the disappointments and incomparable misfortunes of the world that were lived out here in silence. Krisztina walks around the house. The silence, the scent of the thorny southern plants, the warm, sweet-smelling haze that envelops everything like a linen bandage for damaged souls, all this moves me deeply, too. For the first time, I sense that Krisztina is not totally with me, and from somewhere far, far away, at the beginning of time, I hear the wise, sad voice of my father, and it's speaking of you, Konrad." For the first time he utters the name of his guest, without anger, without agitation, in a tone of neutral courtesy. "And the voice is saying you are not a real soldier, you are another kind of man. I do not understand, I still don't know what being different means . . . it takes a long time, many lonely hours, to teach myself that it is always and exclusively about the fact that between men and women, friends and acquaintances, there is this question of otherness, and that the human race is divided into two camps. Sometimes I think these two camps are what define the entire world, and that all class distinctions, all shades of opinion and all variations in power relations are simply variants of this otherness. So just as it is blood alone that binds people to defend one another in the face of danger, on the spiritual plane one person will struggle to help another only if this person is not 'different,' and if quite aside from opinions and convictions they share similar natures at the deepest level. . . .

"There in Arco I understood that the celebrations

were over, and that Krisztina too was 'different.' And I remember the words of my father, who was not a great reader of books, but whom loneliness had taught to recognize the truth; he knew about this duality, he too had met a woman whom he loved profoundly but at whose side nonetheless he remained alone because they were two different people—for my mother, too, was 'different,' just as you and Krisztina are. . . . And in Arco something else became clear to me, as well. The feeling that bound me to my mother and to you and to Krisztina was always the same, a longing, a hope in search of something, a helpless, sad yearning. For we always love the 'other,' we always seek it out, no matter what the circumstances and sudden changes in our lives. . . . The greatest secret and the greatest gift any of us can be offered is the chance for two 'similar' people to meet. It happens so rarely—it must be because nature uses all its force and cunning to prevent such harmony—perhaps it's that creation and the renewal of life need the tension that is generated between two people of opposite temperaments who seek each other out. Like an alternating current . . . an exchange of energy between positive and negative poles, think of all the despair and the blind hope that lie behind this duality.

"In Arco I heard my father's voice and understood that I had inherited his fate, that I was of the same kind he was, whereas my mother, you, and Krisztina stood on the far bank beyond our reach. . . . One can achieve everything in life, wrestle everything around one to the ground, life can offer up every gift, or one can seize them all for oneself, but one cannot change another's tastes or inclinations or rhythms, that essential otherness, no matter how close or how important the bond. That is what I feel for the first time in Arco as Krisztina is walking around the house in which her mother died."

He lets his head drop, leaning his forehead on his hand with the gesture of helpless resignation of a man finally faced with the evidence of the intractability of human relations.

"Then we come home from Arco and start our lives here," he says. "The rest you know. It was you who introduced me to Krisztina. You never let drop the slightest hint that you were interested in her yourself. Our meeting, to me, was unmistakably the most significant thing that had ever happened to me.

She was of very mixed descent, with German, Italian, and Hungarian blood in her veins. Perhaps also a trace of Polish, on her father's side of the family ... she was quite uncategorizable, beyond race or class, as if nature for once had tried to create a self-sufficient, independent, free creature untrammeled by family or social position. She was like an animal: her protected upbringing, her boarding school, her father's culture and delicacy, had all shaped her behavior, but underneath she was wild and untamable. Everything that I could give her, my fortune and social position, was really not of great importance to her, and because of her need for freedom, which was so fundamental, she could not make herself a part of my social world. ... Her pride, which was quite different from that of people who parade their position, their family ties, their wealth, their place in society, or their particular personal talents—Krisztina's pride rested on her splendid independence, which coursed in her as both an inheritance and a poison. She was, as you well know, an inborn aristocrat, and that is something very rare these days: you find it as seldom in men as in women. It is not a question of family or social position. It was impossible to offend her, there was no situation from which she shrank, she tolerated no kind of limitations. And there was something else that is rare in women: she understood the responsibility to which she was committed by her own inner sense of self. Do you remember—yes, of course you do—our first meeting in the room with the table where her father's music sheets lay: Krisztina came in, and the little room was filled with light. She didn't just bring youth with her, she brought passion and pride and the sovereign self-confidence of her unsuppressed nature. Since then I have never met a single person who responded so completely to everything: music, an early morning walk in the woods, the color and scent of a flower, the well-chosen words of an intelligent companion. Nobody could stroke a beautiful piece of cloth or an animal like Krisztina. Nobody took such pleasure in the world's simple gifts: people, animals, stars, books—everything interested her, not in any exaggerated way, not with a pedantic outpouring of learning, but with the unprejudiced joy of a child reaching for everything there is to see and do. As if everything in the world was relevant to her, you know? Yes, you do know.

. . . She was unprejudiced and open and humble because she recognized what a blessing life was. I still see her face sometimes," he says confidingly.

"You won't find any portrait of her in this house, there are no photographs of her, and the large painting of her done by the Austrian, which used to hang between the portraits of my parents, has been taken down. No, you will not find any picture of her here anymore," he says, with a kind of satisfaction, as if reporting on a small act of heroism. "But sometimes I still see her face when I'm half asleep, or when I walk into a room. And now, while we're talking about her, we two who knew her so well, I see her face as clearly as I did forty-one years ago, on that last evening as she sat between us. For you know, that was the last evening that Krisztina and I dined together. Not only was it your last dinner with Krisztina, it was mine also. That was the day when everything happened that was inevitable between the three of us. And as we both knew Krisztina, certain decisions were inevitable: you left for the tropics, Krisztina and I did not speak again. Yes, she lived for another eight years. We both lived here under one roof, but we could no longer talk with each other," he says calmly, and looks into the fire.

"That is how we were," he says simply. "Gradually I came to understand a part of what had gone on. There was the music. There are certain elements that recur in people's lives, and music in my life was one. Music was the bond between my mother, Krisztina, and you. It must have spoken to you in some way that is beyond words or actions, and it also must have been the conduit through which you communicated with each other—and this conversation, this language of music which the three of you shared, was inaudible to us others, to my father and me. That is why we were lonely even when we were with you. But because music spoke to both you and Krisztina, you could continue to communicate with each other even after all conversation between her and me had been silenced. I hate music." His voice rises, and for the first time this evening he speaks with a hoarse intensity. "I hate this incomprehensible, melodious language which select people can understand and use to say uninhibited, irregular things that are also probably indecent and immoral. Watch their faces and see how strangely they change when they're listening to music. You and Krisztina never sought out music—I do not remember you ever playing four-handed together, you never sat down at the piano in front of Krisztina, at least not in my presence. Evidently her sense of tact and shame restrained her from listening to music with you while I was there. And because music's power is inexpressible, it seems to carry a larger danger in that it has the power to arouse the deepest emotions in people who come together to listen to it and discover that it is their fate to belong to each other. Do you not agree?"

"Yes, I do," says the guest.

"That eases my mind," says the General politely. "Krisztina's father also thought so, and he really was a connoisseur of music. He was the only person to whom I once, just once, spoke about all this, about music, about you and Krisztina. He was already very old; he died shortly afterwards. I had returned from the war. Krisztina had already been dead for ten years. Everyone who had ever mattered to me—my father, my mother, you, Krisztina—was gone. The only two people still alive were Nini, my nurse, and Krisztina's father, both of them with that remarkable strength and indifference that old people have, and some mysterious purpose still in life . . . like the two of us today. Everyone was dead, I myself was no longer young, more than fifty years old, and as lonely as that tree in the clearing in my forest, the one left standing when a storm felled all the surrounding timber on the day before war broke out. That one tree remained standing in the clearing, near the hunting lodge. Now, almost fifty years later, a new forest has grown up around it. It, too, is one of the ancients, after an act of will, which nature calls a storm, destroyed everything that had once surrounded it. And out of sheer will, inexplicably, the tree is still alive.

"What is its purpose? . . . It has none. It wants to stay alive. Maybe life and every living thing have no other purpose than to live as long as possible and renew themselves. So I came back from the war, and I talked to Krisztina's father. What did he know about the three of us? Everything. And he was the only one to whom I ever told everything that was possible to tell. We sat in his dark room, surrounded by old furniture and instruments, there were bookshelves and cupboards bursting with scores, music fixed in sign language, trumpet blasts in print, drum rolls on paper, all the music in the world was lying silently in wait in that room, which smelled so old, as if all human life had been sucked out of it. . . . He listened to me, and then he said, 'What do you want? You survived.' He spoke like a judge pronouncing sentence and also bringing an accusation . . . staring half-blind into the room; he was already very old, over eighty. Then I understood that a survivor has no right to bring a complaint. Whoever survives has won his case, he has no right and no cause to bring charges; he has emerged the stronger, the more cunning, the more obstinate, from the struggle. Just as we have," he says dryly.

They measure each other in a glance.

"Then he died, too, Krisztina's father. There was only my nurse and you, somewhere out there in the world, and this castle, and the forest.

"I had also survived the war," he says with satisfaction. "I didn't seek out death, I never went to meet it: that is the truth, there's no other way I can say it. Evidently I still had things I wanted to settle," he continues reflectively. "People were dying all around me, I have seen every variety of death, and sometimes I was amazed at its endless possibilities, for death has its element of fantasy, just as life does. By official count, ten million people died in the war. A world-engulfing fire had broken out and blazed and roared until one sometimes thought that all personal doubts and questions and struggles must be entirely consumed in it . . . but that was not the case. In the midst of this immense human agony, I knew that I still had something private to settle, and that is why I was neither a coward nor a hero, as the book says; I was calm both in storm and in battle, because I knew that nothing bad could happen to me. And one day I came home from the war, and then I waited. Time passed, the world has exploded in a new conflagration and I am certain that it is the same torch as before that has suddenly flamed up again . . . and what smouldered on in my heart was the question that neither the soot nor the ashes of time and war could cover. People by the millions are dying again, and yet you found your way from that far bank where you belong and through this world gone mad to come home and settle the things with me that we could not settle forty-one years ago. Such is the force of human nature—it must provide or receive an answer to whatever is the defining question of a lifetime. That is why you have come back, and that is why I have waited for you.

"Perhaps this world is coming to its end," he says quietly, drawing an arc through the air with his hand. "Perhaps lights are going out all over the world just as they did today across this little part of it; perhaps some elemental event has taken place that is not merely the war, but something more; perhaps something has found its time in us as well, and now it's being settled with steel and fire, where once it was settled with words. There are many signs. . . . Perhaps," he says matter-of-factly. "Perhaps this entire way of life which we have known since birth, this house, this dinner, even the words we have used this evening to discuss the questions of our lives, perhaps they all belong to the past. There's too much tension, too much animosity, too much craving for revenge in us all. We look inside ourselves and what do we find? An animosity that time damped down for a while but now is bursting out again. So why should we expect anything else of our fellow men? And you and I, too, old and wise, at the end of our lives, we, too, want revenge. . . . Against whom? Each other? Or against the memory of someone who is no longer with us? Pointless. And yet it burns on in our hearts. Why should we expect better of the world, when it teems with unconscious desires and their all-too-deliberate consequences, and young men are bayoneting the hands of young men of other nations, and strangers are hacking each other's backs to ribbons, and all laws and conventions have been voided and instinct rules, and the universe is on fire? . . . Revenge. I came back from a war in which I could have died, yet didn't, because I was waiting for my opportunity to take revenge. 'How?' you may ask. 'What kind of revenge?' I can see from your face that you do not understand this need. 'What revenge is still possible between two old men who are already waiting for death? Everyone is dead, what point is there in revenge?' you seem to be saying. And this is my answer: Yes—revenge. That is what I have lived for, for forty-one years, that is why I neither killed myself nor allowed others to kill me, and that is why I have not killed anyone myself, thank heaven. The time for revenge has come, just as I have wished for so long. My revenge is that you have come here across the world, through the war, over mine-infested seas, to the scene of the crime, to answer to me and to uncover the truth together. That is my revenge. And now you must answer."

The last words are almost whispered. The guest has to lean forward in order to hear properly.

"It may be that you are right. Ask. Perhaps I can answer you."

The candles dim, and the dawn wind rustles through the great trees in the garden. The room is now almost completely dark.

19

"There are two questions you must answer," says the General, also bending forward. He sounds as if he is whispering a confidence. "Two questions I formulated long ago in the years I was waiting for you, and that only you can answer. I can see you think I would like to know if I was wrong or not, that you really did intend to kill me that morning on the hunt. If it was not just a figment of my imagination, because after all, nothing happened, and even the best huntsman's instinct may play tricks on him. And you think the second question is: Were you Krisztina's lover? Did you betray me, as the phrase goes, and did she betray me, in the usual wretched sense of the word? No, my friend, neither of these questions interests me anymore. You have answered them yourself, time has answered them since, even Krisztina answered them in her fashion. I have all your answers. You gave yours when you fled the town the day after the hunt and abandoned the colors, as men used to say when they still believed in the true meaning of those words. I'm not asking that question, because I know for certain that you wanted to kill me that morning. I'm not accusing you—in fact, I sympathize with you. It must be a terrible moment when a man is driven to pick up a gun and kill the person closest to him out of whatever sense of need. That's what happened to you in that second. You don't dispute it? . . . You have nothing to say? It's too dark for me to see your face, but it hardly makes sense to send for fresh candles now, the time for revenge has come and we can understand and recognize each other even in the shadows. The time has come and we need to get through it. All these years I have never doubted that you wanted to kill me, and I've always pitied you. I know what you felt so exactly that I could have been standing in your place during that terrible instant when you were overwhelmed. Night had not yet given up its terrors, the underworld still had an open gateway into our world of day, dawn was just about to break, and for a moment you were transported right out of yourself. Such a terrifying temptation. I recognize it. But that's all the stuff of a police report, do you see? ... What would I do with the kind of facts required for a day in court, when mine are in my heart and in my head? What would I do with memories of some musty alcove, the sultry secrets of a bachelor's apartment or the decayed remains of an adultery or the intimate memories of a dead woman and two old men stumbling toward the grave? What a poor, pathetic trial it would be, if now, at the end of our lives, I wanted to take you to court for adultery and attempted murder and I tried to force a confession out of you at a point when the law would regard the act or the not-quite-act as having long since passed the statute of limitations? It would be mortifying, and unworthy of both of us and our youth and our friendship. And perhaps it would make you feel better to recount it all, or what facts there are to recount. But I don't want you to feel better," he says calmly. "I want the truth, and that doesn't lie in a few long-out-of-date facts and the private passions and errors of the body of a woman long since dead and turned to dust. . . . What is all that to me anymore, me the husband, you the lover, now that her body no longer exists and we have grown old? We will talk these things through once more, try to establish the truth and then go to our deaths, I in this house, you somewhere else, in London or the tropics. At the end of our lives, what do truth and falsehood count, or deceit, betrayal, attempted murder, or actual murder, or the question of where, when, and how often my wife, the love and hope of my life, betrayed me with my closest friend? You talk about all these sad and demeaning things, you admit everything, you tell exactly how it began, what kind of envy, jealousy, anxiety, and sadness drove you into each other's arms, what you felt when you embraced her, what feelings of guilt and revenge filled Krisztina's body and mind all those years . . . you could do all that, but what would any of it be worth? At the end it all becomes very simple, what was and what might have been. What was once is not even dust and ashes now. What once made our hearts burn until we thought we would either die or have to kill someone—and I know that feeling, I, too, knew that terrible temptation, shortly after you left, when I was alone with Krisztina—all that is less than the dust the wind blows across the graveyards. It is humiliating and pointless even to mention it. And anyway, I know it all so exactly that I might have read it in a police report. I could recite you the trial evidence like a lawyer at the hearing: And then? What would I do with the secrets of a body that no longer exists? What is fidelity, what do we expect of the woman we love? I am old, and I have thought a great deal about this too. Is the idea of fidelity not an appalling egoism and also as vain as most other human concerns? When we demand fidelity, are we wishing for the other person's happiness? And if that person cannot be happy in the subtle prison of fidelity, do we really prove our love by demanding fidelity nonetheless? And if we do not love that person in a way that makes her happy, do we have the right to expect fidelity or any other sacrifice? Now, in my old age, I would not dare answer these questions as unequivocally as I would have done forty-one years ago, when Krisztina left me alone in your apartment, where she had been so often before me, where you had assembled all those objects in order to receive her, where two people close to me betrayed and deceived me so vulgarly, so ignominiously, and—as I realize now—with such banality. That is what happened." His voice is indifferent, almost bored.

"And what people call 'deceit,' the sad and banal rebellion of a body against a situation and a third person—in retrospect is almost alarmingly a matter of indifference, almost the source of pity like a quarrel or an accident. I did not understand this back then. I stood in your secret apartment as if I were taking in the details of a crime, I stared at the furniture, the French bed. . . . When one is young and one's own wife deceives one with the only friend who is closer than a brother, it is natural to feel that the world has crashed around one. It is inevitable, because jealousy, disappointment, and vanity are all excruciating. But it passes . . . not consciously, and not from one day to the next. Years later, the fury is still there—and yet finally it is over, just as life will be one day. I went back to the castle, to my room, and waited for Krisztina. I waited to kill her or to have her tell me the truth so that I could forgive her. I waited until evening, then I went to the hunting lodge, because she had not come. Which was perhaps childish. . . . Now, looking back, when I want to pass judgment on myself and others, I see this pride, this waiting, this departure, as somewhat childish. But that's how things are, do you see, and neither reason nor experience can do much to change one's stubborn nature. You, too, must know this now.

"I went to the hunting lodge not far from the house—you know it well—and I did not see Krisztina for eight years. The first time I saw her again one morning was as a corpse, when Nini sent word that I could return to the house because she was dead. I knew that she was ill, and as far as I know she was taken care of by the best doctors, who came and stayed here in the castle for months and did everything to save her. As they put it, 'We have done everything within the scope of modern medicine.' Those are just words. They apparently did everything within their erratic knowledge and the limits of their vanity. Every evening for eight years, I was informed of what was going on in the castle, both before Krisztina was ill and then later, when she decided to become ill and die. I do believe such things can be decided—and now I am quite certain of it. But I couldn't help Krisztina because there was an unpardonable secret between us of the kind that it is better not to force open prematurely, because there is no telling what still may be hidden underneath. There are worse things than suffering and death . . . it is worse to lose one's self-respect. That was why I was so afraid of the secret between the three of us. Self-respect is the irreplaceable foundation of our humanity; wound it, and the hurt, the damage, is so scalding that not even death can ease the torture. Vanity, you say. Yes, vanity . . . and yet self-respect is what gives a person his or her intrinsic value. That is why I so feared this secret, that is why people accept the compromises they do, even cheap and cowardly ones.

"Look around you and you will see nothing but partial solutions: this one leaves the woman he loves out of fear of a secret, that one stays and says nothing and waits unceasingly for an answer. . . . I have seen such things. And I have experienced them, too. It is not cowardice, it is one's will to life summoning its last line of defense. I went home, I waited until evening, then I moved to the hunting lodge and waited eight years for something, anything: a word, a message. But Krisztina did not come. In a carriage, the journey there from the castle takes two hours. But to me, these two hours, these twelve miles, were a greater distance in time and space than the tropics to you. That is a given in me, that is how I was raised, that is how things unfolded. Had Krisztina sent a message—any message—her wishes would have been granted. Had she wanted me to fetch you back, I would have set out to search the world for you and bring you back. Had she wanted me to kill you, I would have gone to the ends of the world to find you and kill you. Had she wanted a divorce, I would have given her a divorce. But she wanted nothing. Because she, too, had a strong personality, as a woman, and she, too, had been wounded by those she loved: by this one because he fled from love, not wishing to be consumed by a fateful liaison; by that one because he knew the truth, waited, and said nothing. Krisztina, too, had character, in a different sense of the word from the one we men use. In those years, you and I were not the only ones to whom things happened: they happened to her, too.

"Destiny brushed against me and fulfilled itself, and all three of us had to bear the brunt. For eight years, I did not see her. For eight years, she did not summon me. Just now, while I was waiting for you so that we could discuss what had to be discussed one day, since there is so little time left, I learned something from my nurse: I learned that Krisztina asked for me when she was on her deathbed. Not for you. . . . And I do not say that with satisfaction— nor without it, either, kindly note. She asked for me, and that is something, if not much. . . . But she was already dead when I saw her again. Beautiful even in death. Still young, unmarred by solitude, not even illness had touched that special beauty or spoiled the reserve and quiet harmony of her face. But that is not your affair," he says, suddenly haughty.

"You were living out there in the world, Krisztina died. I was living in lonely affront, Krisztina died. She answered both of us in her way; because the dying always give the right and the final answer— sometimes I think they are the only ones who can do that. What else could she have said after eight years except by dying? Who could say more? She had answered all the questions you or I could have put to her, should she have wanted to speak to either of us. The dead give the final answer. She did not want to speak to us. Sometimes I think that of the three of us, she was the one who was betrayed. Not I, whom she deceived with you; not you, who deceived me with her—deceit, what a word! There is a vocabulary that defines a human situation that is so soulless and mechanical, but when it's all over, as it is for the two of us now, there is not much we can do with such a vocabulary. Deceit, infidelity, betrayal—mere words, when the person involved is dead and has already addressed their true meaning. Beyond words is the mute reality that Krisztina is dead—and we are still alive. When I understood this, it was already too late. All that was left was the waiting and the thirst for revenge—and now that the waiting is over and the time for revenge is here, I am amazed to feel how hopeless it all is, and the pointlessness of anything we could learn or admit or fight out between us. I understand the reality. Time is a purgatory that has cleansed all fury from my memories. Now I sometimes see Krisztina again when I'm asleep—and also when I'm awake—walking through the garden with a big straw hat, slender, in a white dress, coming out of the greenhouse or talking to her horse. I see her, I saw her this afternoon while I was waiting for you and fell asleep for a moment. I saw her as I was dozing," he says shamefaced, an old man. "I saw pictures from long, long ago. And this afternoon my mind grasped what my heart has known for a long time: infidelity, deceit, betrayal—I understood them, and what can I say? . . . We age slowly. First, our pleasure in life and other people declines, everything gradually becomes so real, we understand the significance of everything, everything repeats itself in a kind of troubling boredom. It's the function of age. We know a glass is only a glass. A man, poor creature, is only a mortal, no matter what he does. Then our bodies age: not all at once. First, it is the eyes, or the legs, or the heart. We age by installments. And then suddenly our spirits begin to age: the body may have grown old, but our souls still yearn and remember and search and celebrate and long for joy. And when the longing for joy disappears, all that are left are memories or vanity, and then, finally, we are truly old. One day we wake up and rub our eyes and do not know why we have woken. We know all too well what the day offers: spring or winter, the surface of life, the weather, the daily routine. Nothing surprising can ever happen again: not even the unexpected, the unusual, the dreadful can surprise us, because we know all the probabilities, we anticipate everything, there's nothing we want anymore, either good or bad. That is old age. There's still some spark inside us, a memory, a goal, someone we would like to see again, something we would like to say or learn, and we know the time will come, but then suddenly it is no longer as important to learn the truth and answer to it as we had assumed in all the decades of waiting. Gradually we understand the world and then we die. We understand phenomena and the motive forces of men and the sign language of the unconscious. People communicate their thoughts in sign language, have you noticed? As if they were discussing important matters in a foreign language like Chinese, which had to be translated into the language of reality. They have no self-knowledge. All they talk about is what they want, thereby exposing themselves unconsciously in all their hopelessness.

"Life becomes almost interesting once one has learned to recognize people's lies, and one starts to enjoy the comedy as people keep saying things other than they think and really want. . . . That is how we arrive at the truth, and truth is synonymous with old age and death. But it doesn't hurt anymore. Krisztina deceived me, what a foolish word! And with you of all people, what a pitiful rebellion! Don't look at me like that: I'm saying it in sympathy.

"Later, when I had more experience and understood everything, because time washed up the telltale flotsam of this shipwreck onto my lonely island, I looked back into the past with pity and saw you two rebels, my wife and my friend, wracked with guilt and self-recrimination, wretchedly unhappy in the heat of your defiant passion, rise up against me, in a life-and-death struggle.

"Poor things! I thought, more than once. And I imagined the details of your rendezvous in a house on the edge of a small town, where secret meetings are almost impossible, being penned together as if onboard a ship, while at the same time being painfully on view. A love that knows no moment of peace, because every step, every glance, is watched with concealed distrust by lackeys, servants, and everyone around you. The trembling, the constant game of hide-and-seek with me, those fifteen stolen minutes under the pretext of a ride or a game of tennis or music, those walks in the forest where my gamekeepers keep watch over every kind of game. . . . I imagine the hatred in your hearts when you think of me, when every step you take brings you up against my authority, the authority of a husband and landowner and aristocrat, against my social and financial ascendancy, against the whole crowd of my servants, and against the strongest force of all: the dependence that forces you to acknowledge, beyond love and hate, that without me you can neither live nor die. You unhappy lovers, you could deceive me, but you could not elude me: I may be a different kind of man, and yet the three of us are as inextricably attached as crystals in the laws of physics. And your hand on the gun goes weak one morning when you want to kill me, for you can no longer bear all this torment, all the hiding, all the misery. . . . what else could you do? Run off with Krisztina? You would have to resign your commission, Krisztina is also poor, you cannot accept anything from me. No, you cannot run away with her, you cannot live with her, you cannot marry her, to remain her lover is to be exposed to a danger worse than death, because you must constantly anticipate being denounced and unmasked, you must fear having to fight a duel with me, your friend and your brother. You will not hold out for long against such danger. And so, one day when the time is ripe and somehow palpable between us, you raise your gun; and later, whenever I think of that moment, I feel genuine pity for you. It must be the hardest and most agonizing of tasks to kill someone dear to you," he says parenthetically.

"You are not strong enough to do it. Or the ideal moment passes and you can no longer do it. There is such a thing as the perfect moment—time brings things of its own accord, we do not merely insert acts and phenomena into time. A single moment, a particular point in time may offer a possibility—and then it's gone and there's nothing more you can do. You let the hand holding the gun drop. And next day you leave for the tropics."

He inspects his fingernails with care.

"But we stay here," he says, still looking at his fingernails, as if this were the important thing, "we, Krisztina and I, stay here. We are here, and everything comes to light in the secret but orderly way that messages travel between people, in waves, even when nobody mentions the secret or betrays it. Everything comes to light because you have gone away and we have stayed here, alive, I because you missed your moment or your moment missed you—it comes to the same thing—and Krisztina because, first of all, there is nothing else she can do, she has to wait, if only to find out whether we have kept silent, you and I, the two men to whom she is bound and who are avoiding her: she waits to find out the meaning of this silence, and to understand. And then she dies. But I remain here, and I know everything, and yet there is one thing I do not know. And now, the time has come for me to have a response. Answer, please.

"Did Krisztina know, that morning on the hunt, that you wanted to kill me?"

The question is framed matter-of-factly, but there is a pitch of tightly wound curiosity in his voice, like that of children begging the grown-ups to tell them the secrets of the stars and other worlds.

18

The guest does not move. His elbows are on the chair arms, and he's holding his head in his hands. Finally, he takes a deep breath, bends forward, and rubs a hand over his brow. He is preparing to speak, but the General cuts him off.

"Forgive me," he says. "You see, now I've said it." He rushes on, as if to excuse himself. "I needed to say it, and now that I've done so I feel that I'm not asking the right question and that I'm making things painfully awkward for you, because you want to tell me the truth but I have phrased the question incorrectly. It sounds like an accusation. And I am obliged to admit that, as the decades passed, I could not shake the suspicion that the moment in the forest at dawn was neither the result of sheer chance nor an opportunistic impulse nor a consequence of urgings from the other world.

"No, what torments me is the suspicion that other moments preceded this one, and that they were moments of absolutely sober calculation in the clear light of day.

"Because when Krisztina learned that you had fled, what she said was, 'Coward.' That was all, and it was the last word I ever heard her utter; it is also her final judgment on you. And I am left with this word. Coward. Why? . . . I rack my brains, later, much later. A coward about what? About life? About our life as a trio or about your separate life together? Too much of a coward to die? Too much of a coward to live with Krisztina and too much of a coward to die with her? Not enough will power? . . . My mind goes around and around. Or too much of a coward about something else? Not life or death or flight or betrayal or stealing Krisztina from me or renouncing her—no, simply too much of a coward to commit a straightforward act worked out in discussions between my wife and my best friend but likely to be uncovered by the police? And did the plan fail because you were too much of a coward? . . . That is the question to which I would like an answer before I die. But I did not ask it correctly just now, forgive me; it's why I did not allow you to speak when I saw that you wanted to answer me. From the standpoint of humanity and the universe it's insignificant, but to me it is of capital importance. I am one solitary human being, the person who accused you of cowardice is now mere ashes and dust, and I would like to know, once and for all, what it was that you were too much of a coward to do. Your answer will draw a line under my questions and allow me to know the truth, and if I do not know the absolute truth about this one detail, then I know nothing at all.

"For forty-one years my life has been suspended between an everything and a nothing, and the only person who can help me is you. I do not wish to die like this. And it would have been better, and more worthy, if forty-one years ago you had *not* been a coward, as Krisztina made clear; it would have been more worthy if a bullet had extinguished what time could not, namely the suspicion that the two of you colluded in a plan to murder me but that you were too much of a coward to carry it out. This is what I would like to know. Everything else is mere words, deceptive shapes: 'lies,' 'love,' 'misdeeds,' 'friendship,' all of them pale under the intense light of this question, bleached of life like the bodies of the dead or pictures subject to the ravages of time. None of it interests me anymore, I have no desire to know the truth about your relationship, any of the details, the 'hows' and the 'whys.' I do not care. Between any two people, a woman and a man, the 'hows' and the 'whys' are always so lamentably the same . . . the entire constellation is despicably straightforward. 'Because' and 'like that'—something could happen, something did—that is what makes the truth. Finally, there is no sense in investigating the details. But one has an obligation to seek out the essentials, the truth of things, because otherwise, why has one lived at all? Why has one endured these forty-one years? Why, otherwise, would I have waited for you—not in your guise of a faithless brother or a runaway friend but in mine of both judge and victim, expecting the return of the accused? And now the accused is sitting here, and I pose my question, and he wishes to answer. But, have I posed it correctly, have I said everything he needs to know, as both perpetrator and accused, if he is to speak the truth? Because, you know, Krisztina gave her own answer, and I don't mean the act of dying.

"One day, years after her death, I found the diary bound in yellow velvet that I had searched for that night—the night after the hunt that was the turning point in your life—in the drawer of her desk. The book had vanished, you left the next day, and I never exchanged a word with Krisztina again. Then she died. You were living in some far-off place, and I was living here in this house, because after her death I moved back so that I could live and die in the rooms where I had been born and where my ancestors had lived and died before me. That is how it will be, for things have a rhythm and order of their own, regardless of our wishes. And even the book in its yellow velvet binding, Krisztina's strange 'book of honor' with its alarming evidence of her inner self and her love and her doubts, went on living in its mysterious way, right out there in the open. It lived on, and I found it one day, much later, among her things, in a box in which she had put the ivory miniature of her mother, her father's signet ring, a dried orchid that I had given her, and this little book tied in a blue ribbon and sealed with her father's ring.

"Here it is," he says, pulling it out of his jacket and holding it out to his friend. "This is what remains of Krisztina. I have never cut the ribbon, because she left no written authorization for me to do so, and so I had no means to know whether her confession from the other side of the grave was addressed to me or to you. It is to be assumed that the book contains the truth, because Krisztina never lied." His voice is severe, and respectful.

But his friend does not reach for the book.

Head in hands, he sits motionless, staring at the thin, yellow-velvet-bound book with the blue ribbon and the blue-wax seal. His body is absolutely still; not even an eyelid flickers.

"Would you like us to read Krisztina's message together?" asks the General.

"No," says Konrad.

"Would you not like to, or would you not dare to?" the General says with the cold arrogance of a superior officer addressing his junior.

Their eyes meet over the book and stay locked.

The General keeps holding it out to Konrad, and there is no tremor in his hand.

"I decline to answer this question," says the guest.

"I understand," says the General, and in his voice there is a strange hint of satisfaction.

With an almost lazy gesture, he throws the little book into the embers of the fire, which begins to glow darkly as it receives its sacrifice, then slowly absorbs it in a welling haze of smoke as tiny flames lick up out of the ashes. They sit and watch, still as statues, as the fire comes to life, flares as if in pleasure at the unexpected booty, then begins to pant and gnaw at it until suddenly the flames burst upwards, the wax seal is melted, the yellow velvet burns in an acrid cloud, and the pages, aged to the color of ancient parchment, are riffled by an unseen hand; there, suddenly, in the blaze is Krisztina's handwriting, the spiky letters once set on paper by fingers now long since dead, and then letters, paper, book, all turn to ashes like the hand that once inscribed them. All that is left in the embers is ash, black ash, with the sheen of a mourning veil of watered silk.

They watch, wordless, the play of light on the blackness of the ash.

"And now," says the General, "you may answer my question. There are no witnesses anymore who could testify against you. Did Krisztina know that you wanted to kill me that day in the forest? Will you give me an answer?"

"No, I shall no longer answer that question either," said Konrad.

"Good," says the General dully, almost with indifference.

19

The room is now cold. It is not yet daybreak, but the half-open window admits a breath of dawn air, fresh, carrying a faint hint of thyme. The General shivers as he rubs his hands.

It is the hour before sunrise, and both men look suddenly ancient, as yellowed and bony as the rattling inhabitants of a charnel house.

With a mechanical gesture, the guest abruptly raises his hand and looks in exhaustion at his wristwatch.

"I think," he says softly, "that we have talked

about everything that needed to be talked about. It's time I went."

"If you would like to go," says the General politely, "the carriage is outside."

Both men get to their feet and move spontaneously toward the fireplace to warm their thin hands at the embers of the dying fire. Only now do they become aware of how cold they are: the night has been unexpectedly chilly and the storm that extinguished all the lights in the nearby power station passed very close to the castle.

"So you are going back to London," says the General, almost to himself.

"Yes," says the guest.

"You are going to live there?"

"Until I die."

"Yes," says the General. "Of course. Would you not care to stay until tomorrow? Have a look at things? Meet someone? You haven't seen the grave. Or Nini, indeed," he adds politely.

He speaks haltingly, as if seeking the right words for his farewell but failing to find them. But his guest remains calm and cordial.

"No," he says politely. "There is nothing, and no

one, that I wish to see. Please give my regards to Nini."

"Thank you," says the General, and they go to the door.

The General reaches for the handle, and they stand facing each other as social politeness demands, a little stooped, ready to say their farewells. Both take a last glance around the room, as if knowing that neither of them will ever set foot in it again. The General blinks, and seems to be looking for something.

"The candles," he murmurs distractedly as his glance falls on the smoking stubs in their holders on the mantel. "Look at that, the candles are burned right down."

"Two questions," says Konrad abruptly, his voice flat. "You mentioned two questions. What is the other one?"

"The other one?" They are leaning toward each other like two accomplices afraid of the night shadows and hidden listeners in the dark. "The second question?" the General repeats in a whisper. "But you haven't answered the first one yet. . . . Look, Krisztina's father's reproach was that I had survived. What he meant is that things always survive. One doesn't answer only with one's death, although that is a perfect answer. One also answers with one's life. Both of us survived her. You, by leaving; I, by staying. Out of cowardice or obliviousness, calculation or grievance, we survived. Do you think we were justified? Don't you think we have a responsibility to her beyond the grave, because she in her humanity amounted to more than the two of us put together? More, because she died, thereby answering to us, whereas we lived on, and there's no way to prettify that.

"These are the facts. Whoever survives someone is a traitor. We had the feeling that we had to survive, and there's no prettifying that, for she died because of it. She died because you went away and because I stayed but never once went to her, and because we—the two men to whom she belonged—were more despicable and proud and cowardly and arrogant and silent than a woman can bear; we ran away from her and betrayed her by our survival. That is the truth, and that is what you have to know in London, in the last hours of your lonely life. And here in this house I have to know it too: I know it already. Surviving someone whom one loved enough to consider killing for, who was life and death to one, may not be defined as a capital offense, but it is, nonetheless, a criminal act. It is not recognized as such in the law, but we recognize it," he says dryly, "and we know that all our offended, cowardly, haughty masculine intelligence has won us nothing at all, because she is dead and we are alive, and the three of us always belonged together, in life or in death. It is a very hard thing to understand, and once one does, one is overcome by the strangest sense of unease. What did you hope to achieve by surviving her, what victory did you win? . . . Did you spare yourself some horrible awkwardness, some painful situation? What awkwardness or painful situation could matter, when what is at issue is the very truth of your existence, because somewhere on earth there is a woman who matters to you, and this woman is the wife of the man who also matters to you. . . . Does public opinion carry any weight in something like this? No," he says simply.

"Finally, the world is irrelevant. All that counts is what remains in our hearts."

"In our hearts?" asks the guest.

"The second question," says the General, his hand still holding the door. "Namely, what did we win with all our intelligence and our pride and our presumption? Has the true meaning of our lives not been the agony of longing for a woman who is dead? It's a hard question, I know. I cannot answer it. I have done everything, seen everything, and yet this I cannot answer. I have seen peace, I have seen war, I have seen the glitter of empire and utter human misery, I have seen your cowardice and my own arrogance, I have seen combat and surrender. Yet I think that, at bottom, perhaps the significance of everything we did was in the ties that bound us to one particular person—ties, passion, call it what you will. Is that the question? Yes. I want you to tell me." His voice drops as if to foil some hidden listener behind him.

"What do you think? Do you also believe that what gives our lives their meaning is the passion that suddenly invades us heart, soul, and body, and burns in us forever, no matter what else happens in our lives? And that if we have experienced this much, then perhaps we haven't lived in vain? Is passion so deep and terrible and magnificent and inhuman? Is it indeed about desiring any one person, or is it about desiring desire itself? That is the question. Or perhaps, is it indeed about desiring a particular person, a single, mysterious other, once and for always, no matter whether that person is good or bad, and the intensity of our feelings bears no relation to that individual's qualities or behavior? I would like an answer, if you can," he says, his voice louder and more imperious.

"Why do you ask me?" says the guest quietly, "when you know that the answer is yes."

Their eyes measure each other, steadily, unblinking.

The General takes a deep breath and pushes down the handle of the door. The great stairwell is filled with surging shadows and the flicker of lights. They walk down in silence. Servants hurry to meet them with candles and the guest's coat and hat. Outside the big double doors, wheels grind and crunch on the white gravel. The men take leave of each other with a handshake, a deep bow, wordlessly.

20

The General walks toward his bedroom. At the far end of the corridor, Nini is waiting.

"Are you feeling calmer now?" she asks.

"Yes," says the General.

They walk side by side, the nurse with quick little steps, as if she had just got up and was hurrying to her first morning tasks, the General slowly, leaning on his stick. They move through the picture gallery. When they come to the bare space on the wall where Krisztina's portrait once hung, the General stops.

"Now you may hang it up again."

"Yes," says the nurse.

"It's of no importance anymore."

"I know."

"Good night, Nini."

"Good night."

The nurse stands up on tiptoe, lifts her little hand with the yellowed skin lying in creases over the bones, and traces the sign of the cross on the old man's forehead. They give each other a kiss. It's an awkward, brief, odd kiss, and if anyone were there to see it, it would provoke a smile. But like every kiss, this one is an answer, a clumsy but tender answer to a question that eludes the power of language.